Parents I Need You,
Now I am Adolescent

PRSE
of the Book

"A book of great inspiration, courage, and hope, every word rings with truth, kindness, and the beauty of the human spirit."

— Greenman Vijaypal Baghel
Renowned Environmentalist/Honored as Social Reformers of
India by Wikipedia

"We don't always get to choose what happens in this life, but we can choose to grow in compassion and wisdom as a result. This book offers valuable, practical methods for doing so."

— Dr. Roopinder Dogra
MBBS, DNB (Obstetrics & Gynaecology) and Author of
"Prisms of Life"
(Currently actively practicing in Kuwait)

"What a beautiful, rich, and wise book on parenting. I wish I could give a copy to every new parent on the planet."

— Dinesh Verma
Author & CEO, Gullybaba Publishing House Pvt. Ltd.

This book is selected by National Book Trust(NBT), Government of India at:
▶ Beijing International Book Fair (China), 2018

PARENTS
I NEED
YOU,
NOW I AM
ADOLESCENT

Learn about the Tools and Techniques
to be a happy parent of your Adolescent

Gullybaba Publishing House Pvt. Ltd.

GULLYBABA PUBLISHING HOUSE PVT. LTD.

ISO 9001 & ISO 14001 Certified Co.

Regd. Office: 2525/193, 1st Floor, Onkar Nagar-A, Tri Nagar, New Delhi-110035 (Near Kanhaiya Nagar Metro Station)

Branch Office: 1A/2A, 20, Hari Sadan, Ansari Road, Daryaganj, New Delhi-110002

Ph.: 9350849407, 011-27387998

E-mail: info@gullybaba.com

Websites: GullyBaba.com, GullybabaKids.com

Revised Edition: 2019

ISBN: 978-93-81970-07-2

Copyright© 2019, Publisher

Contents

Few Words

E arly adolescence can be a challenging time for children and parents alike. Parents often feel unprepared and they may view the years from 10 through 14 as a time just "to get through." During the early adolescent years, parents and families can greatly influence the growth and development of their children.

Adolescence is a time of rapid and dramatic change. Parents can see these changes in the way teenagers behave, express their feelings and in the way, they interact with their families. Parents need to adapt their parenting style to suit the changing needs of their children. Knowing about the changes that adolescents experience will help you to understand and manage your teenager more effectively.

Adolescent children are, nonetheless, children. It's not good to try to push them into being grown up too soon, and it is not good to try to turn them into the babies they once were. Accepting them for who and what they are usually works out well. Loving them for who they are or even in spite of it always works out well. There is one final thing about adolescent children that parents need to understand: For all the parents who will tell their tales of woe about their adolescent children, there are many, many, parents who will tell you that they had absolutely no problems or no difficulty understanding their young son or daughter.

This work will provide a helping hand to parents who are in need to understand their adolescent.

– Dinesh Verma

Acknowledgements

I acknowledge the almighty GOD or universal energy which has brought precious words of wisdom in front of my eyes, the wisdom to touch the soul of those words and creativity to present some of them to parent in YOU.

Out of the large repository of words few words I would like to acknowledge:

When I first helped my newborn son, I looked at him with tenderness and wondered and thought to myself, you are the most precious gift from God. I don't own you. I am here to help you find your way, to love you, and to let you go.

Susie Risho, Mother of Three Grown Boys

And I am a practising parent trying to touch the soul of above words.

I would like to put in my appreciation and acknowledgement for my family members, relatives, friends and Team of Gullybaba Publishing House Pvt. Ltd. and GullybabaKids.com.

I convey my special thanks to all the kids with whom we experimented and played activities and all those who entertained and taught me.

No work can find success without the most important part, that is, YOU, The READERS. I wholeheartedly thank all those who took pain in the making of the book.

-Dinesh Verma

Some cautions while handling the Adolescents

A dolescents' sensitivity and understanding to clinch a great deal has been a national endeavour to enhance education, especially in country's middle class gentry.

Parents lacking the necessary homework may view their children aged between 10 to 14 years as a time just "to go ahead."

In the early phase of adolescence, parents and family elders can influence the growth and development of their children in a major way.

Adolescence: The Period of Sense and Essence

From birth to death, human beings pass through different phases of life. Adolescence, among these phases, is found to be the most sensitive and easily persuasive phase of life that starts in biology and ends in society. Of course, adolescence may be defined as the period when human being remains in the middle path of saying goodbye to childhood and stepping into the ladders of adulthood. In this phase, a person's cognitive, psychological, and social characteristics experience a constant change from childish traits to those of adulthood. This period also remains to be a big challenge for adolescents as they require adjustment to changes in the self, in the family, and in the peer group. In contemporary society, they also experience institutional changes. In the initial stage of adolescence, a change is experienced in school setting that usually involves a transition from elementary school to junior high school or middle school; and in the final phase of adolescence there is experienced a transition from high school to a wide world of activities that gradually include college and university life and then taking care of one's own children.

If viewed rationally, the phase of adolescence for both adolescents and their parents is a period of thrills and thoughts. It includes the essence of joys and obstacles; it also consists of discovery and astonishment;

and of leaving the past behind and yet of establishing links with the future. Thus, adolescence can be a period of confusion— for the adolescent experiencing this phase of life; for the parents who are nurturing the adolescent during his or her progression through this period; for other adults charged with encouraging the evolution of youth during this period of life and disturbing, phenomenally unprecedented frequency—for adolescents who find themselves playing parental role rather than that of the offspring which they had been till recently before becoming parents of their children.

BANGS, NO BOUNCES

"The well-being and welfare of children
should always be our focus."
~ *Todd Tiahrt*

It's not easy to become a perfect parent of an adolescent. Such parenthood may sometimes make the parents' eyes moist with sympathy. When they find the images of bedrooms in which their adolescent child's homework assignments get mingled up with potato chips wrappers, dirty socks and school bags scattered like anything futile objects to be set by his/her parents, especially mother.

Nevertheless, parents' botheration about their child's well-being goes more meticulous than messy bedrooms. They remain apprehensive about the difficulties that young adolescents often face. They remain vulnerable to strong emotions, rebellious attitude, peer pressures, weaker motivation, relationships, attraction towards the opposite sex, drugs, alcohol, suicides and so on.

Between 10 to 14 years of age, children undergo physical, emotional and mental changes. If combined together, these changes can shake the balance of young teens' and their parents' lives miserably. It may create major obstacles in the health and career of teenagers who already remain on the verge of failure in their school and result mockery made for such failure.

In other perspective, if you discuss with adults who work with young adolescents — teachers, school counsellors and principals — you will get another view about these children. It will not be wrong to say that young adolescents are susceptible to challenges and frustrations, which suffice to put the parents on litmus test of their patience. It's also an undeniable truth that these same adolescents can also be funny, aspiring, enthusiastic and interested to learn something valuable. According to some research, most young teenagers try to bang and go with a bang to mark their presence rather than letting their target missed as bouncing balls. They (and their parents) sometimes bark up the wrong tree, but they get through the young adolescent years successfully and grow into adults who find work, establish important relationships and become ideal citizens of their country.

This phase of life is relatively easier when parents, families and caretakers learn as much as they can about this time in children's lives and when they give their children the support they need. This book has been designed to make this endeavour fructuous. It brings together the information from scientifically based research, as also from interviews with award winning middle school teachers, counsellors and principals — most of whom also are — or have been recently — parents of such children who remain in their teens. This book stands as a guide to answer the following questions and concerns that parents of young adolescents often need to clear:

- How can my child change from 10 to 14 years of his/her age?
- What should I do to be a perfect parent for my adolescent?
- How should I communicate better with my child?
- To what extent should I given liberty to my child?
- How should I help my child infuse more confidence in himself/herself?
- How should I help my child establish good friendships and cope with detrimental peer pressure?

- What should I do to keep the media remaining least influential in leading my child to wrong way?

- What is school like for adolescents?

- How can I stay best-involved in my child's school and in other activities?

- How should I infuse in my child, the significance of healthy competition?

- How should I keep my child away from stress and feelings of envy etc?

- How should I help my child develop interest for successful studies?

- How should I keep instill in my child the sense of motivation to learn and excel, both in and out of school?

- What should I do to help my child develop good values and learn to distinguish right from wrong?

- Up to what extent my child should go into social media networking?

- How should I tell — and what can I do — if my child happens to face a serious difficulty of any form?

This phase of life is easier when parents, families and care takers learn as much as they can about this time in children's lives and when they become a source of support to children.

✗ ✗ ✗

TRANSFORMATIONS

> "Spread love everywhere you go; first of all in your house. Give love to your children, to your wife or husband, to a next door neighbour. Let no one ever come to you without leaving better and happier."
> ~*Mother Teresa*

How will my child transform from the age of 10 to 14?

Growth and transformation are an integral part of our lives, but during early adolescence the rate of transformation or change is well evident. We consider 10-year-olds to be the children just above the phase of infancy; we regard 14 year- olds as "almost adults". We welcome the transformations as a journey towards the phase of adulthood, but we also find them a bit disturbing. When children are younger, it is easier to predict the time and pace of transformation in them. But by the initial stage of adolescence, the bond between a child's real age and his developmental landmarks grow weaker. Like many things: for example, genes, families, friends, neighbourhoods, values and other forces as experienced in social life.

Physical Transformations: As the children enter puberty, the young teens undergo many conspicuous physical changes, not only in size and shape, but also in such things as the growth of pubic and underarm hair and increased body odour include the development of breasts and the beginning of menstruation; for boys, the development of testes.

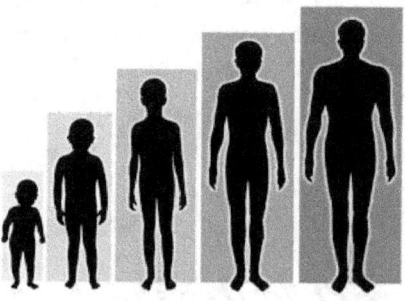

All adolescents do not begin puberty at the same age. Among girls, it may happen anywhere from the age of 8 to 13; while among boys, on average, it takes place about two years later. This is phase of life when students' physical traits vary the most within their classes and among their friends – some may grow so faster, by the end of school year, they may be too large for the desks they were assigned in earlier. Others may transform into shape so slowly that they would look much younger to the children of their age.

With this natural process, early adolescence often brings new concerns about body image and appearance.

Both girls and boys who never took care of their looks may suddenly turn more concerned about primping, worrying and complaining about being too short, too tall, too fat, too skinny, too dusky or too pimply. Growth of body parts vary from individual to individual and time to time. For example, hands and feet may grow faster than arms and legs. Since the movement of their bodies requires coordination of body parts — and since these parts are of changing proportions — young adolescents may look clumsy and awkward in their physical activities.

The degree of growth at which physical changes and development take place can also influence other parts of the adolescents' life. An 11-year-old girl who has recently entered the phase of puberty will have different interests than those of a girl who does not do so until she reaches 14. Young teens that bloom too early or too late may have special concerns. Late bloomers (especially, boys may feel boys) may feel they are unable to compete in sports with more physically developed classmates. Early bloomers (especially girls) may fall under pressure in adult situations before they are emotionally or mentally able to take care of them. The combined effect of the age in the initial stage for physical changes in puberty and the ways in which friends, classmates, family members and the world around them respond to those changes can haveprolong effects on an adolescent. Some adolescents, however, like the idea of developing differently from their contemporaries. For example, they may enjoy some advantages, especially in sports, over classmates who mature later.

Irrespective of speed of growth, many young teens have an impractical view of themselves and need to be reassured that differences in growth speeds are normal.

Emotional Transformations: The majority of experts believe that the notion of young teens being controlled by their "raging hormones" is overstated. Nevertheless, this age can be one of mood swings, sulking, and a desiring privacy and being tetchy. Young children are unable to think far ahead, but young teens can and they do — which allows them to think over their future. Some may worry much about:

- their performance in school;
- how they appear, how is their physical development and how popular they are;
- the imminent death of a parent;
- being bullied at school;
- violence in their school;
- having no friend;
- drugs and alcohol;
- starvation, poverty and unemployment in the country;
- their inability to get employed;
- their country's vulnerability to nuclear bombs and terrorists attacks;

- the separation (divorce) of their parents; and

- dying.

There are several young teens who are very self-conscious. And since they are experiencing spectacular physical and emotional transformations, they are often overly sensitive about themselves. They may be pensive about personal qualities or "defects" that merit vital importance to them, but are hardly noticeable to others. (Belief: "I can't attend the party tonight because *everyone* will make mockery of this baseball- sized zit on my brow." Facts: The pimple is very small and covered by hair). An adolescent can also be trapped in himself. He may believe that he is the only individual who feels the way he feels or has the same experiences, that he is so special that no one else, especially his family, can understand him. This belief can contribute to feelings of loneliness and isolation. Besides, a young teen's focus on him has implications for how he mingles up with family and friends. ("I *can't* be seen going to watch a movie with my *mother/father!*").

Adolescents' emotions often seem to be beyond limits. There is found no consistency in their actions. It is normal for young teens to swing regularly from being glad to being sad and from feeling smart to feeling dull. Actually, some regard adolescence as a second phase of toddlerhood. As a middle school counsellor in Mumbai, says, "One minute, they want to be treated and taken care of like a small child. Five minutes later they are pushing adults away, saying, 'Let me do it.' It may help if you can help them understand that they are in the midst of some major changes, changes that don't always move steadily ahead."

Besides the changes in their emotions that they have, most young teens adopt different ways to express their emotions. For example, a child who greeted friends and visitors with fervent hugs may turn into a teen who gives these same people only a small wave or affirmative nod. In the same way, hugs and kisses for a parent may be replaced with a pulling away and an, "Oh, Mom!" It's worth remembering, though, that these are usually the transformations in *ways of expressing* feelings and not the actual *feelings* about friends, parents and family members.

So, just try to have a look at extreme emotional swings or consistent despondency in your child. These can suggest severe emotional upheavals.

Cognitive Transformations: The cognitive or mental transformations that occur in early adolescence may be a bit difficult to see, but they can be just as spectacular as physical and emotional changes. During adolescence, most teens make huge leaps in the way they think reason and learn. Younger children are required to see and touch things to believe that they are real. But in early adolescence, children become able to think about ideas and about things that they unable to see or touch. They become better able to think though problems and see the consequences of different perspectives or actions. For the first time, they can think about the consequence, instead of what is. A 6-year-old thinks that a person with a smile is happy and a person with tears in his eyes is sad. A 14-year-old may tell you that a sad person smiles to hide his true feelings which he does not want to reveal.

The cognitive transformations help young teens to learn more advanced and complicated things in school. They become curious to attain and apply knowledge and to go for a range of ideas or options. These mental transformations also carry over into their emotional lives. Within the family, for example, the ability to reason may change the way a young teen speaks to and acts around his parents. He starts anticipating how his parents will react to something he says or commits and prepares an explanation for his defence.

Besides, these mental transformations make adolescents to regard who they are and who they may be. This process is called *identity formation* and it is a conspicuous activity during adolescence. Most adolescents will explore a spectrum of possible identities. They go through the "phases" that to a parent can seem to be ever-changing. Of course, adolescents who don't go through this phase of exploration are at relatively major risk of developing psychological problems, especially depression, when they become adults.

After setting their feet in adulthood, they with more experience and cognitive maturity can endeavour with their different roles, adolescents struggle in developing a sense of who they are. They start realising that they act (treat) differently with different people: son or daughter, friend, teammate, student, worker, professional and so forth.

Though young teens start regarding themselves more as adults, they still do not have the experience and maturity required to act like adults. Resultantly, their behaviour may be out of step with their ideas. For example, your child may participate enthusiastically in a march to raise money to save the environment, but while he may litter the road with biscuits wrappers or soda cans. It is also possible that he may spend an evening on the phone or exchanging e-mails with a friend talking about how he does not like a classmate because he is a gossipmonger.

Thus, it is time consuming for young teens and their parents to adapt to all these transformations or changes. However, the changes are also exciting. They allow a young teen to envision what he can be in the future and to chalk out the plans to become the person of aspiration.

They start realising that they act (treat) differently with different people: son or daughter, friend, teammate, student, worker, professional and so forth.

✗ ✗ ✗

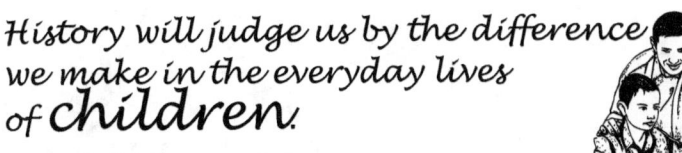

History will judge us by the difference we make in the everyday lives of children.

-Nelson Mandela

BEING A WORTHY PARENT

"Listen to the desires of your children. Encourage them and then give them the autonomy to make their own decision."
~*Denis Waitley*

Reckoning with Parenting Attributes

The process of parenting goes biologically and socially. It's the term summarising the set of behaviours involved across life in the relations among organisms who are usually non-specific, and typically members of different generations or, at the least, of different genealogical backgrounds. This may include all those who are a part of the years when the child grows, not only the biological parents. Parenting interactions provide resources across the generational groups and function in regard to domains of survival, reproduction, nurturance, and socialisation.

In this way, parenting is a multifaceted process, involving much more than a mother or father providing food, safety, and support to an infant or child. Parenting involves bidirectional relationships between members of two (or more) generations; can extend through all or major parts of the respective life spans of these groups; may engage all institutions within a culture (including educational, economic, and socio-political ones); and is embedded in the history of a people—as that history is made within the natural and designed settings within which the group exists. Given, then, the temporal variation that constitutes history, the variation of culture and of its institutions that exist in various physical and designed ecological niches, and the variation, within and across generations, in strategies for and behaviours designed to be congruent with these niches, we may note that *diversity* is a key substantive feature of parenting behaviour. Focus on this variation, instead of central tendencies, is crucial in order to understand parenting well. Apart from it, there are multiple levels of organisation that change in and through integrated, mutually interdependent or "fused" relationships that occur over both ontogenetic and historical period. As such, *context*, as well as diversity, is a principal feature of parenting.

Today, the major challenge with the adolescents are that they cannot dispense with their parents, they cannot even move ahead smoothly without the guidance of their parents. Thus, they remain in need of parenting that promotes their positive development and widens their avenues in every sphere of life.

Sequentially, the human ecological point-of-view provides understanding of the levels, networks, or social systems or subsystems within which person-context relations take place. This point-of-view provides developmentalists with an understanding of the dynamics of person-context relations getting established within a specific setting (e.g. the home) within which a person develops (a microsystem); the interconnected set of specific systems (e.g., the home, the classroom, the neighbourhood) within which the person develops (the mesosystem); the settings (termed the "exosystem") in which the person does not interact (e.g. the workplace of a young child's parent) but wherein developments occur (e.g., the experience of job-related stress) that influence behaviour in the micro- or meso- system; and the broad social institutional context (the macro system) that, by virtue of its cultural and public policy components, textures social commerce and influences all other systems embedded within it.

The adolescent grapple with the challenges and stress that may influence the emotional character of interactions with his child, and the child may carry the "residue" of his interaction at home with the parents into the child's interactions with peers in the classroom.

Thus, it is obvious that there are significant interconnections between the life-span, the life-course, and the human ecology point of views. All viewpoints focus on the linkages existing between transformations within a person over the course of his/her life and the transformational structure and function of his/her family, peer group, school, workplace, and community setting, which in turn are entrenched within policy, cultural, and historical contexts. All perspectives are concerned with the manner in which the pattern or system of these relations shape human development over the course of life. Therefore, there are various factors that influence behavioural repercussions among adolescents.

A kind of noticeable diversity is found in children's social context relations. As a result of their characteristics of individuality, children elicit differential reactions in their parents, and these reactions provide the basis of feedback to the child, i.e. there appears reactionary stimulation which influences his/her further individual development. The parent tries to mould the child as per his/her desire, but part of what determines the way in which the parent does, and then this is none other than the child himself/ herself.

Moreover, the child-parent relationship is embedded in social networks which, in turn, are embedded in hitherto larger community, societal, cultural, and historical strata of organisation. Time—history—cuts through all the systems; however, change is a perennial phenomenon.

Parenting: The Way of Child's Upbringing, Socialisation, and Parent-Adolescent Relationships

The main concern and duty of a child's parent or elders are to raise the young person in as healthy way as possible. The parents' role is to provide the child with a safe, secure, nurturant, loving, and supportive ambience that can allow them to have an enjoyable and healthy youth. This kind of experience allows the youth to increase their knowledge, values, attitudes, and behaviours necessary to evolve into an adult making a fructuous contribution to self, family, community, society and above all, humanity in general.

Fulfilment of these "duties" by parents is termed *parenting*. In other words, parenting is a term that summarises behaviours used by a person—usually. But, of course, not exclusively, the mother or father—to raise a child. Given the above-described characteristics of this set of activities, it is obvious that parenting is the main concern and duty of a parent or elders in the family.

Notwithstanding this factuality, it is also evidenced that adolescents live in different family structures. So for an adolescent, it vitally important to understand all these influences and the effect and value of all such relationships. And parents thus have a major role to play in this process.

What should I be a worthy parent for my early adolescent child?

When the children reach the phase of middle grades, parents generally start lessening their involvement in the lives of their children. However, your young adolescent needs as much concern and affection from you as he needed at the time of her/her infancy — and maybe more as well. A healthy relationship with you or with other adults is the best safeguard your child has as he grows and explores the world of his choice. By the time he enters into the phase of adolescence, you and he will have had years of experience with each other. So, the parent of today's toddler may also become the parent of tomorrow's teenager.

There may arise a change in the relationship betw you and your child — in fact, it almost certainly must change — however, as he develops the skills required to become a successful adult. These changes can be worthwhile and well-attributable in some sense. As your middle school child makes mental and emotional leaps, your interactions and talks will grow richer. As his interests develop and deepen, he may start teaching *you* — how to hit the target, what is happening with the city municipality or current wave in the country or why a new movie is worth watching.

Children in the early phase of adolescence need adults who can stand beside them – those who can connect with them, communicate with them, spend time with them and evince a genuine interest in them.

In India, we find the people with a great variety of attitudes, opinions and values. They have different notions and preferences, which can affect our way of choice to raise our children. Across these differences, however, research has shown that being worthy parents requires the following attributes:

- **Showing affection:** We turn angry when our children behave badly and we admonish them at least. We may also feel dejected as we become angry or upset. But expression of these feelings does not mean that we do not love our children. Young adolescents need adults who are there for them — people who connect with them, communicate with them, spend time with them and evince a genuine interest in them. This is how they learn to care for and turn affectionate to others.

- **Extending Support:** Young adolescents need support as they cope with the problems that may appear insignificant to their parents and family elders.

They expect praise from us when they do their best. They need encouragement to develop interests and personal qualities.

- **Determining Limits:** Limits, usually determined by parents/family elders, rarely let the children experience the deprivation of physical and emotional security. Ritu Chandra, a former middle school principal, elucidates it as thus, "They need parents who can say, 'No, you cannot go to the mall all day or to movies with that group of kids." Psychologist Diana Manchanda identifies three types of parents: *authoritarian, permissive and authoritative.* By studying about findings from more than 20 years of research, she and her colleagues have noticed that to be worthy parents, it's best to avoid extremities. *Authoritarian* parents who lay down hard-and-fast rules and expect their children to always do as they are instructed or *permissive* parents who have very few rules or regulations and give their children too much liberty are most likely to have the toughest time as parents. Their children are susceptible to a spectrum of negative behavioural and emotional repercussions. However, *authoritative* parents, who set limits that are clear and come with explanations, tend to put less efforts for their adolescents. "Do it because I said so" probably didn't work for your son/daughter when he was 6 and it's even less likely to work now that he/she's become an adolescent.

• **Being a Role Model:** A role model in young adolescents' life is a great source of guidance and adoption of some ways or manners or styles etc. as a role model's actions exert great influence upon them. Similarly, your actions speak louder than words. If you set high standards for yourself and treat others with kindness and respect, your child stands a better chance of following your example. As adolescents explore possibilities of which they may become, they look to their parents, peers, well-known personalities and others to define who they may become.

- **Teaching Responsibility:** By birth, we are not aware of how to act responsibly. A sense of responsibility comes in course of time or as we face the circumstances in life. As children grow up, they need to learn to take more and more responsibility for such things as:

  - completing chores, like doing yard work, cleaning their rooms or assisting to cook food that contribute to the family's well being;

  - accomplishing homework without getting irritated

  - embarking on community welfare activities;

  - exploring ways to be helpful to others in need; and

  - accepting both the good and bad decisions that they make.

- **Providing a Spectrum of Experiences:** Adolescence is a period of exploring numerous areas and doing new things. Your child may go for new sports and new academic pursuits and study new books. He may experiment different forms of art, learn about different cultures and career options and participate in community or religious activities. Within your limited resources, you can open avenues for your child. You can introduce him to new people and new worlds. In this pursuit, you may renew in yourself long-neglected interests and flairs, which can also set a good example for your child. Don't get desperate when you see in his interests.

* **Giving Respect:** It is appealing to label all young adolescents as being tough and rebellious. But these youngsters vary as much as do children in any other age group. Your child needs to be treated with respect, which requires you to recognise and appreciate her/his differences and to treat him as a respectable human being. Respect also requires you to show your concern by trying to see things from your child's preference and to consider his needs and feelings. By treating your young adolescent with respect, you help him attain pleasure in good behaviour.

No parent can claim to be hundred per cent perfect in parenting. However, a bad decision or an "off" day (or week or month) isn't likely to have any lasting impact on your child. What merits the most important thing lies in being a worthy parent is what you do over time.

If you set high standards for yourself and treat others with compassion and respect, your child is sure to have a better chance of getting into your footsteps.

✗ ✗ ✗

"A nurturing parent protects and teaches their child to survive and thrive in the kind of society in which they will live."

COMMUNICATION

"The relation between parents and children is
essentially based on teaching."
~*Gilbert Highet*

How should I communicate effectively with my child?

When your child is a pampered individual, he may not often be a great communicator, particularly with his parents and other family elders who love him a lot. If Mahatma Gandhi said, "Home is the first school for a child," his sentence has many latent meanings and lessons. The point to say is that children not only learn how to read and write at home but also learn the mannerism, social etiquette and communication skill at home by watching the activities and interactions of their parents and family elders. But it also happens with the children that they try to conceal what they have done at schools as Rabindra Ghosh, a middle school teacher in Kolkata, explains: "They don't necessarily want to tell you what they did at school today."

It has been the observation of many psychologists that when parents remain aware of where their children are and what they are doing (and when the adolescent knows that parent knows what psychologists call *monitoring*), adolescents are less susceptible to a range of bad experiences, including drug, alcohol and tobacco use; sexual behaviour and suicide; and delinquency and violence. The key, according to psychologists, is to be inquisitive but not interfering, working to respect your child's privacy as you establish trust and proximity.

If you develop this habit at the time when your child is little, it will be so easy for you to communicate with a young teen. A school counsellor explains, "You don't suddenly dive in during the seventh grade and say, 'So what did you do with your friends on Saturday night?'" But it's not impossible to improve communication when your child reaches the early phase of adolescence. Here are some tips:

- **Make it sure that there is no written guideline for result-oriented communication:** It doesn't mean that if a child talks about what's important, will always work with another one. One middle school teacher and mother of two says her daughter is open and talkative, while her son is quieter. But since her son likes music, writing and reading, this mother often goes with him to a local bookstore. Here, in a place where he's comfortable, the son describes stories and book characters as a link to what he is thinking and feeling. By listening to music with him and proofreading his writing when he's willing to let her, this mother encourages her son to move ahead with better tempo.

- **Listen:** "You cannot understand your child until you listen to him/her." So such situation will often prevail when you will to talk less and listen more to your child. To listen means to avoid interrupting and paying close attention. This is best done in a quiet place with no distractions. It's difficult to listen attentively if you're also with some important chores. Often just talking with your child about a problem or an issue helps to make the things clear. Sometimes the less you offer advice, the more your young teen may ask you for it. Listening can also be the best way to uncover a more serious problem that necessitates your attention.

Sometimes the less you offer advice, the more your young teen may ask you for it.

- **Create opportunities to talk:** If you want to communicate with your child, the most necessary thing is that you need to make yourself available for the purpose.

Young adolescents hardly follow fix or "scheduled" talks; they don't open up when you tell them to, but they do when *they* want themselves. Some teens like to talk when they first get home from school. Others may like to talk at the dinner table or at bedtime. Some parents talk with their children in the car, preferably when the radio, tapes and CDs aren't playing. "I take my daughter to a mall — not the closer one, but the cooler one that is an hour and a half away," says a middle school teacher and mother. Majority of best conversations grow out of shared activities. "Parents try to grab odd moments and have this deep communication with their child," remarks Neha Kumar, a teacher. "Then they are frustrated because it doesn't happen."

- **Discuss over differences:** Sometimes, parents are unable to continue the communication as they find it difficult to manage the differences with their child. It's often easiest to demarcate these differences when you have put in place clear expectations. If your 13-year-old daughter knows she is supposed to be home by 9:30 p.m. — and if she is aware of the consequences for not meeting this curfew — the likelihood that she will be home on time increases.

Differences of viewpoints are easier to manage when we recognise that these differences can provide good opportunities for us to rethink the demarcations and to negotiate new ones, a skill that is valuable for your child to develop. For example, when your daughter is 14, setting a later curfew for some occasions may be fine.

Such conversations are viable by virtue of your child's growing cognitive skills and ability to reason and consider many possibilities and views. Since she can consider that her curfew should be later on the weekend than on school nights, your insistence that "it doesn't matter" will only create a discord.

When differences arise, apprise your child of your concerns firmly but politely that can prevent the differences from evolving into ruckus. Explaining *why* your child made or wants to make a low profile choice is more constructive: "Dropping out of your algebra class will cut off lots of choices for you in the future. Some colleges won't admit you without two years of algebra, plus geometry and some trigonometry. Let's get you some help with algebra."

When differences arise, apprise your child of your concerns firmly but politely that can prevent differences from evolving into ruckus.

- **Abstain from over-reacting:** Responding too strongly can lead to yelling and screaming and it can bring the conversation to its premature end. "Try to keep anxiety and emotions out of the conversation — then kids will open up," suggests eighth-grade teacher Laxman Subramanyam from Kerala. Instead of getting irritated, he says, "It's better to ask, 'What do you think about what you did? Let's talk about this'."

A Middle school teacher Sumit Patel enunciates, "Kids are more likely to be open if they look at you as somebody who is not going to spread their secrets or get extremely upset if they confess something to you. If your kid says, "I've got to tell you something. Saturday night I tried beer,' and you go off the deep end, your kid won't tell you again."

While judging themselves critically, adolescents make themselves vulnerable when they open up to parents. We know that the best way to encourage a behaviour is to reward it. If you are critical when your teenager talks to you, what he sees is that his openness gets punished rather than rewarded.

- **Discuss the things that merit importance to your young teen:** Different youngsters like to discuss different things. Some of the things they discuss may not seem of any worth to you, but, as school counsellor Sushma Chaterjee explains, "With kids, sometimes it's like a different culture. You need to try to understand this, to put yourself in their place and time." She cautions against pretending to be thrilled about something that creates monotony in you. By asking questions and listening, however, you can show your child that you consider his feelings and opinions. Here are the topics that generally interest young adolescents:

  - *School:* If you inquire of your child, "What did you do in school today?" he most probably will answer, "Nothing." Of course, you know that it's not true. By having a glance of your child's assignment book or reading notices sent home by the school, you will know that on Tuesday, your 10-year-old began studying animals in Asia that are headed for extinction or that the homecoming football game is on Saturday night. With this information, you then can ask your child about specific classes or activities, which is more likely to create an ambience of starting a talk with him/her.

  - *Hobbies and interests:* If your child likes sports, discuss on his favourite team or event or watch the World Series or the Olympics with him. Most young adolescents are interested in music, that too the latest ones. Babita Shah, a middle school teacher in Pune remarks that "Music has been the signature of every generation. It defines each age group. Parents ought to at least know the names of popular singers." It's important, however, to tell your child when you believe that the music he is listening to is inappropriate — and simultaneously give the reasons behind its being so. If you do not tell it, your silence can be misconstrued as approval for him.

- *Emotions:* As discussed earlier, young adolescents remain anxious about several different things. They worry about: their friends, being popular, sexuality, being overweight or scrawny, tomorrow's math test, grades, getting into college, being abandoned/ isolated and the future of the world. The list goes endless. Sometimes it's difficult to know whether a problem seems huge to your child. School counsellor Neeraj Sharma says that if he is unsure, he asks, "Is this a small problem, a medium problem or a big problem? How important is it to you? How often do you worry about it?" Determining the size and enormity of the problem helps him decide how to tackle it.

- **Family:** Young adolescents prefer talking about and engage themselves in making plans for the whole family, such as vacations, as well as the things that influence them individually, such as curfews or allowances. If you need back surgery, your child will want to know ahead of time. He may also want to learn more about the operation. Being a part of the discussion on such topics can contribute to your child's feelings of belonging and security.

- **Sensitive subjects:** It's families' duty to handle the sensitive issues in a way that is consistent with their importance. Remember, though, that abstaining from such issues won't release them from its tangle. However, if you avoid discussing with your child on sensitive issues, he may turn to the media or his friends to obtain information. This enhances the chances that what he hears will be out of line with your values or that the information will be wrong — or both.

Reshma Sikander, a middle school teacher from Ludhiana, enunciates that middle schoolers have wrong or inaccurate information about many important subjects. They will say they know about certain sensitive topics but they really don't. Discussing a sensitive subject directly may not work, Ms. Sikander remarks, "You can't just sit down and say, 'Today we are going to talk about marijuana use.' That shuts down the conversation before you ever start."

- ***The lives, hopes and expectations of the parents:*** A majority of young adolescents want a window to their parents' world to meet both of their past and present. How old were you when you got your ears pierced? Did you ever have a teacher who drove you crazy? Did you get an allowance when you were 11? If so, how much? Were you sad when your grandpa died? What is your boss like at work? This doesn't mean you are obliged to dump all of your problems and emotions into your child's lap. You are a parent, not a peer and an inappropriate question must be answered. However, recounting some things about your childhood and your life today can help your child sort out his own life.

- *The future:* With the development of the cognitive abilities of young adolescents develop, they start thinking more about the future and its possibilities. Your child may desire talking more on what to expect in the years to come — life after high school, jobs and marriage. He may put such questions as, "What is it like to live in a college hostel?" "How old do you have to be to get married?" "Is there any chance that the world will be destroyed one day?" "Will there be enough petrol so that I can drive a car when I get older?" These questions deserve the best answers that you can provide (and those that you can't answer deserve an honest, "I don't know").

- *Culture and current events:* We live in a media-dominated world. Even young children are exposed to television, music, movies, video and computer games and other forms of media. Remember, though, that the media can provide a window into your adolescent's world. For example, if you and your child have watched the same movie (together or separately), you can ask him if he liked it and what were parts best liked by you.

'Music has been the signature of every generation. It defines each age group. Parents ought to at least know the names of popular singers.'

- **Communicate with politeness and affection:**
  The words delivered by young teens or anything
  committed by them may be outrageous or low-
  spirited or both. However hard your child pushes
  your buttons, it's best to respond politely. The
  affection and self-control that you display in
  conversations with your child may someday be
  reflected in his talks with others.

  How you say something merits as importance as
  what you say. "Stop picking at your face" can
  bring a young adolescent to tears. "Your room
  looks like a pigsty" isn't as helpful as, "You need to
  spend some time picking up your room. The job
  will be easier if you spend 5 minutes right now
  picking the clothes up off the floor — putting the
  dirty ones in the hamper and hanging the clean
  ones up. After lunch you can spend 5 minutes
  straightening up your bookshelf." Youngsters also
  pay attention to the tone of your voice. A 10-year
  old can easily tell a calm voice from an angry one.

However hard your child pushes your buttons, it's best to
respond politely.

Compassion goes hand-in-hand with affection and
respect. As Anita Damodar, an expert on educating
middle-grade students and the mother of two grown
children, explains, "When I was an active parent and
teacher, I had a rule that grew out of a classroom
experience: 'I will never knowingly be unkind to you and

you will never knowingly be unkind to me.' That turned out to be the most powerful rule I ever set, either in the classroom — it changed the culture — or at home."

Communicating with affection also doesn't call for talking down to adolescents. They are becoming more socially conscious and aware of events in the world and they appreciate thoughtful conversations. Gaurav Aggarwal, a middle school counsellor in Delhi, tells the story of a trip he made with a group of adolescent girls when the state was debating whether to curb the corruption at governmental level. "We were driving along the highway when we got into a big discussion," he recalls. "We got so intense talking about it that we missed the exit to come home."

✗ ✗ ✗

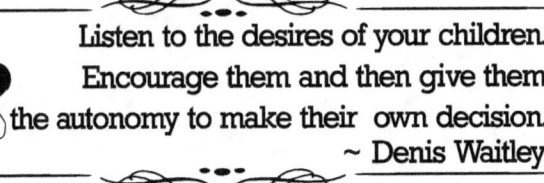

Listen to the desires of your children.
Encourage them and then give them
the autonomy to make their own decision.
~ Denis Waitley

LIBERTY

"The true character of a society is revealed in how it treats its children."
~*Nelson Mandela*

How much liberty should I give to my child?

When children reach the phase of adolescence, they often want more freedom. On the other hand, parents tighten their rope between wanting their children to be confident and able to do things for themselves and knowing that the world can be a scary place with threats to their children's health and security.

There are also such parents who consider giving excess of wrong kind of liberty to their children before their having access to adolescence. Other parents are too strict in this regard, denying young teens both the responsibilities they require to develop maturity and the opportunities they need to make choices and accept their consequences.

According to the research, adolescents do best when they remain closely connected to their parents but at the same time are allowed to have their own opinion and even to disagree with their parents. Here are some tips to help balance closeness and freedom:

- **Set limits:** Children never want setting of limits over them, but they do require them for their own benefits and safety. In a world that can seem too hectic for adults and adolescents alike, limits provide a source of safety. Oftentimes, adolescents whose parents do not set limits feel unloved. Setting limits is most effective and viable when it is done early. However, it is not so difficult or impossible to establish limits during early adolescence.

- **Be clear:** Most young teens respond positively and appropriately to specific instructions, which are repeated regularly. As middle school teacher Reshma Sikander remarks, "Don't just say, 'I want your room clean,' because they don't know what that means. Say, in a non-argumentative way, 'This is how I perceive a clean room.' They may say, 'I don't really want the lamp over here, I want it over there.' Give them the freedom to express themselves."

- **Allow them to make reasonable choices:** Choices enable young teens to become more open to guidance. For example, you can tell your son that his arithmetic homework must be done before bedtime, but that he has a choice of completing it either before or after supper. And you can instruct your 14-year-old daughter not to hang around the video arcade with her friends on Saturday night, but she can have a group of friends over to your house to watch a movie.

Using humour and creativity as you give choices may also make your child more willing to accept them. One middle school teacher couldn't get her own child to hang up clean clothes or put dirty clothes in the laundry basket. So she gave her daughter two options— either all the clothes had to be picked up or everything would go on the floor. "I was washing the clothes, and then putting them in piles on the floor," the teacher recalls. "It made me crazy, but it worked." After two weeks, her daughter got tired of the stacks on the floor and she began picking up her clothes.

- **Give liberty in stages:** When a young teen becomes more responsible and mature, parents give him more privileges and freedom of making a choice. You might first give your young teen the right to choose which sneakers to buy within a certain price range. Later on, you can let him make other clothing purchases — with the understanding that price tags won't be removed until you approve the items. Eventually, you can give him a clothing allowance to spend as he considers.

- **First priority to health and safety:** As a responsible parent, your first priority is to protect your child's health and safety. Your child needs to know that your love for him requires you to veto activities and choices that threaten either of these. So let your child know what things threaten his health and safety — and often the health and safety of others — and put your foot down. Doing this is made more difficult, though, because adolescents have a sense that nothing can hurt them. Simultaneously, he feels that everything he experiences is new and unique, an adolescent also believes that what happens to others will not happen to him. His beliefs are based on the fact that adolescence is the healthiest period of time during our lives. In this period, physical illnesses are not common and fatal disease is rare. The important thing to emphasise to your child is that, while he may be very healthy, death and injury during adolescence are most often caused by violence and accidents more often as a result of negligence.

Your child needs to know that your love for him requires you to veto activities and choices that threaten either of these.

- **Allow not to make choices that reduce future options:** There are some things that aren't worth fighting about. It may affront you if your son wears a shirt to school that doesn't match with his pants, but this isn't a choice that can reduce future possibilities for him. Young teens may have a growing sense of the future, but they still lack the experiences required to completely understand how a decision they make today can affect them in days to come. They may have heard that smoking is harmful to health, but they do not fully understand what it means to die of lung cancer at the age of 45. Talk to your children about the lifelong consequences of choices they make. Help them understand there are right and wrong decisions and that knowing one from the other can make all the difference in their lives. Let your child know that you are "the keeper of options" until he is old enough and responsible enough to assume this responsibility: He may not skip school and he may not avoid taking tough courses that will prepare him for higher studies in higher classes in college and university.

You can guide by being a good listener and by asking questions that help your child think over the results of her actions.

- **Guide, but fight the temptation to control:**
The earlier section on being a worthy parent
elaborated on the importance of striking a good
balance between laying down the law and allowing
excess freedom. With most young teens, it's easiest
to maintain this balance by dint of guidance but not
having control. Young teens need opportunities to
explore different roles, try on new personalities and
experiment. They need to learn that choices have
pleasant results. That means making some
mistakes and accepting the results. But parents
need to provide guidance so that young teens avoid
making too many inferior choices.

Parents can guide by being a good listener and by
asking questions that help their child think about
the upshots of his actions: "What could happen if
you let someone who is drunken drive you home?"
Your guidance may be better appreciated if you
ask your child's advice on a range of matters and
follow the advice if it appears to be reasonable:
"What should we cook for Daddy's birthday?" "I
don't have to work on Saturday. Is there anything
special you'd like to do?"

The cases for different children in respect of fine
line between guiding and controlling may vary.
Some children, whether they are 7 or 17, need
holistic guidance and fewer privileges than do
other contemporaries.

- **Making mistakes by kids a natural
phenomenon:** We often expect from our

children to grow and act like adults who can solve problems and make good choices. These abilities are a critical part of being independent.

To develop these abilities, young teens on occasion may need to fail, provided the stakes aren't too high and no one's health or safety falls at stake. Making mistakes also allows young teens to learn where they have made mistakes and where they need revampation.

It's an arduous task for a child to learn how to pick himself up and start over if his parents always rescue him from adverse situations.

• **Let take actions and have the fates:** If you emphasise your child on returning home by 10 p.m., do not ignore his midnight arrival. You lose credibility with your child if he suffers no fates for returning home two hours late. However, the punishment should fit the crime. Grounding a child for six weeks restricts the entire family. Instead, you might talk with your child about how coming in two hours late has affected you. You've been up worrying and losing your sleep. But you'll still have to get up the next morning at your regular time, make breakfast, do your chores and go to work. Since his lack of consideration has made your life tougher, he will have to complete some of your chores so that you can go to bed earlier the next night.

Your teenager may want to dye his hair with bizarre colour in vogue and pierce most parts of his body, but these acts may be autonomous of his sense of who he is and who he wants to become.

Ultimately and despite what we often hear and read, adolescents look to their parents first and foremost in shaping their lives. When it comes to morals and ethics, political beliefs and religion, teenagers almost always have more in common with their parents than their parents believe. As a parent, you should look beyond the surface, beyond the specific behaviours to who your child is becoming. Your teenager may want to dye his hair with bizarre colour in vogue and pierce most parts of his body, but these expressions may be independent of his sense of who he is and who he will become. At the same time that many of your child's behaviours are finally harmless, some of them may not only be harmful but fatal also.

Parents are supposed to initiate talk with their children and make it clear that many of the major threats to their future health and happiness are not a matter of chance, but are a matter of choice — the choices like drinking and driving, smoking, drugs, sexual activity, and dropping out of school.

According to research, the adolescents who engage in one risky act are more susceptible to participate in others, so parents need to be at the front and centre, talking to their children about the potentially fatal consequences of opening that Pandora's Box.

✗ ✗ ✗

CONFIDENCE

"Parenting makes us better in so many regards."
~*Alissa Quart*

How should I help my child grow his confidence?

Feeling of inadequacy often persists with young teens. They have new bodies and developing minds and their relationships with friends and family members continue to be on ebb and flow. They understand for the first time that they aren't good at everything. The changes in their lives may occur more swiftly than their ability to adjust to them.

Poor self-esteem often peaks in early adolescence, and then improves during the middle and late teen years as identities gain strength and focus. At any age, however, a lack of confidence can be a serious problem. Young teens with poor self-esteem can be lonely, awkward with others and sensitive to criticism and with what they see as their shortcomings. Young teens with low confidence are less likely to join in activities and form friendships. This isolates them further and slows their ability to develop a better self- image. When they do make friends, they are more susceptible to negative peer pressure.

Some young adolescents lacking confidence are held back in class. Others act out to have attention. At its worst, a lack of confidence is often linked with self-destructive behaviour and habits — smoking or drug or alcohol use, for example.

Girls often experience deeper self-doubts than boys do (although there are many exceptions). This can be for many reasons:

- Society makes girls to cherish the notion that it is important for them to get along with others and to be conspicuously slim and pretty. Life can be just as difficult, however, for a boy who thinks he has to meet society's expectations that boys have to be appreciable at sports and other physical activities.

- In course of time however, the norms have changed, and people with a single child or two kids, have instilled a different kind of thinking and upbringing for their girls, but still such thoughts continue to prevail.

- Generally, girls mature physically about two years earlier than boys do, which require girls to deal with issues of how they look popularity and sexuality before they are emotionally mature enough to proceed in this regard.

- Girls may receive confusing messages about the values of achievement. Although girls are made to believe that achievement is important, some also fear that they won't be liked, especially by boys, if they come across as too smart or too capable, especially in the areas of math, science and technology. (This too has changed now, and there is a competitive and die- hard spirit amongst girls also)

In case your young adolescent happens to experience the shock of a severe lack of confidence over long period, he may be cured from this malady consulting a counsellor or other professionals specialised for it. This is especially true if he also has a drug or alcohol problem, a learning disability, an eating disorder or severe depression. Most young adolescents will get through the rough spots with adequate time and support.

As believed by most psychologists, self-esteem and self- confidence represent a range of feelings that a child has about himself in many different situations. Psychologist Susan Harter has developed a theory of self-esteem that considers both a child's sense of confidence in an area of activity and how important that area is to the child. For example, adolescents may think over numerous situations: competing on the track team, studying math, dating, taking care of younger brothers or sisters and so on. An adolescent may feel more confident committing some of these things than others. He may feel immensely good about his athletic flair and skill at math, but doesn't feel good about his dating life. He may also have chequered feelings about how good a sister he is to his baby brother/sister. How good this teenager feels about himself ties to how important each of these areas is to him. If having a very active dating life is the most important area of his life, this boy/girl will not feel good about himself. If being a scholar-athlete is most important area, he will feel very good about himself. Based on this theory, the best ways to help your child develop confidence include the following:

- **Keep your child procured with opportunities to succeed:** As teacher Diana David outlines, "The best way to instill confidence in someone is to give them successful experiences. You need to set them up to succeed — give them experiences where they can see how powerful they are. Kids can engineer those experiences. Part of confidence knows what to do when you don't know what to do."

  Better you help your child build confidence in his abilities by encouraging him to take an art class, act in a play, join a soccer or baseball team, participate in science fairs or computer clubs or play a musical instrument — whatever he likes to do that brings out the best in him.

  Don't thrust upon your child any specific activity

to be accomplished. Most children, whether they are 3 or 13 years old, resist attempts to get them to do things that they don't enjoy. Thrusting children upon participating in activities they haven't chosen for themselves can lead to annoyance. Try to balance your child's experiences between activities that he is already good at doing with new activities or with activities that he is bad at doing.

You can also help your child build confidence by assigning him family responsibilities at which he can succeed — unloading the dishwasher, cleaning his room, mowing the lawn and so on.

- **Help young teens feel safe and trust in themselves:** The adolescents' ability to trust in themselves comes from receiving unconditional love that helps them to feel safe and to develop the ability to solve their own problems. Your child, like all children, will encounter the circumstances that require him to lean on you and others. But always relying on you to bail himself out of challenging situations can stunt his emotional growth. "We have to teach our children how to cope with the things they encounter, instead of easing the path," says teacher Laxman Subramanyam.

• **Discuss the worries related to school violence and global terrorism:** Many children may have witnessed appalling scenes of death and destruction on television and on YouTube. You can help your child understand that though the country has suffered dreadful acts of terror, we are strong people who can come together and support each other cope with the difficult times. Besides, you can also do the following:

- Try to create a calm ambience at your home through your own behaviour. This may not be viable if your family gets affected directly by an act of terror or violence. If you are worried, you need to explain to your child what you are feeling and why. Children take emotional cues from those they love.

- You must listen attentively to what your child says. Assure him that adults are working to make homes and schools safer for children.

- Guide your child to distinguish fact from fiction. Talk about facts with your child and avoid guessing, exaggerating or overreacting.

- Keep monitoring your child's television, radio and Internet activity. Help him avoid overexposure to violent images, which can heighten his anxiety.

- Use historical examples (for example, World Wars or the Columbia space shuttle explosion) to explain to your child that bad things happen to innocent people, but that people go on with their lives and resolve even terrible ordeals.

- Carry on your normal family routines.

• **Appreciate and encourage:** Appreciation is important to adolescents when it comes from those they love and count on most — their parents and other important adults in their lives. Appreciating your child will help him gain confidence. However, the compliments that you give him must be genuine. He will recognize when they are not.

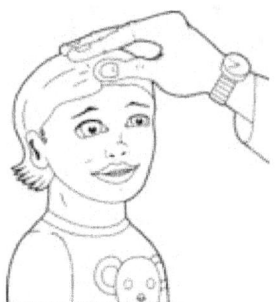

x x x

The solution to every parenting problem starts with nine little words: 'I'm here.' 'I hear you.' 'How can I help?'

FRIENDSHIPS

"The well-being and welfare of children should
always be our focus."
~*Todd Tiahrt*

How should I help my child find good friends and fight detrimental peer pressure?

Our ears keep buzzing with the word 'friend'— friends on WhatsApp; friends on Facebook, friends in school, friends in coaching centre and so on. Thus, friends are the world for adolescents and teenagers.

Sometimes friendships affect many areas of young adolescents' lives — grades, how they spend their time, what clubs they join and how they behave in public places, such as parks, shopping malls and multiplexes. Youngsters who have difficulty in establishing friendships are more susceptible to have poor self-esteem, perform poorly in school, become drop out, get involved in delinquency and suffer from a spectrum of psychological problems as adults.

Irrespective of their ages, children must have a feeling that they fit in — that they belong. As children reach the threshold of the teenage, they need to be "one of the gangs" is stronger than at any other age. Friendships become closer and more significant and play a major role in allowing young adolescents to sort out who they are and where they're proceeding. They are likely to form small groups or cliques, each with a special identity.

Many parents keep worrying that their children's friends will become so influential in their lives that their own roles will be eclipsed. Parents still remain anxious more that their children's friends will encourage them to take part in such activities that are harmful.

As per the studies of the psychologist Thomas Berndt and his colleagues, friends do influence one another's attitudes and behaviour and that, over time, friends become more and more similar in their attitudes and behaviour. For example, adolescents whose friends described themselves as more disruptive in school enhanced in disruption themselves over the school period.

Generally, grade seventh to ninth remains to be the peak period for peer influence. During this phase of life, friends often influence taste in music, costumes or hairstyles, as well as the activities in which youngsters choose to participate. However, peers donot replace parents because parents still remain the greatest influence in child's life. Young teens are more inclined to turn to their parents than to peers for guidance in deciding what post-high-school plans to make, what career to select and what religious and moral values to choose. This influence is greatest when the bond between parent and child is strong.

Here are some tips to guide you in helping your child to form good friendship:

- **Make sure if peer pressure can be good or bad:** Majority of young teens are attracted to friends who are like them. If your child chooses friends who are not interested in school and who perform poorly in their classes, he may be less willing to study or complete assignments. If he chooses friends who like school and perform well in their studies, however, his motivation to get good grades may enhance. Friends who avoid alcohol and drugs will also exert a positive influence on your child.

Young teens are more inclined to turn to their parents than to peers for guidance in deciding what post-high-school plans to make.

- **Try to understand your child's friends:** To learn about your child's friends is to drive them to events — talking with them in the car will reveal many things about them. You can also welcome your child's friends to your home. Make it a comfortable place with food and by creating a convenient atmosphere. Having your child's friends at your home can provide you with peace of mind and allow you to assess their lifestyle and characteristics, as well as help you to gain a better understanding of what they talk about and what they are interested in.

- **Try to understand the parents of your child's friends:** Though you need not be best buddies, it helps you understand attitudes and approaches of others' parents whether their parenting is similar to that of yours. Former principal Ritu Chandra elucidates, "The kid may seem okay, but you need to know if someone is around at the other house to supervise." Understanding others' parents makes it easier to learn what you need to know: where your child is going, which he/she's going with, what time the activity starts and ends, whether an adult will be present and how your child will get to and from the activity.

- **Give your child with some unstructured time in a safe place to hang around with friends:** Activities are crucial, but excess of dance lessons or basketball practices can lead to burnout. Allowing your child some unstructured time with friends in a safe place with adult supervision lets him share ideas and develop important social skills. For example, among friends your child can learn that good friends are good listeners, that they are helpful and confident (but not overly so), that they are fervent, have a sense of humour and that they respect others. Spending time with others may also help your child to change some behaviours that make others uncomfortable around him: being too serious or unenthusiastically critical of others.

- **Discuss with your child on friendship:** You can discuss with your child on how to be a good friend and how all friendships have their pros and cons. You can also discuss on the importance of making good choices when he is with friends. "I always tell them, 'If it feels wrong, it probably is',"

explains teacher Babita Shah. Teacher Sumit Patel guides his middle school students and his own children as thus, "You need to look at who you are when you are with this person." He also suggests that they ask themselves this question: "How do you want to be described by others?" Children's responses can guide their behaviours and lifestyle.

Spending time with others may also help your child change some behaviours that make others uncomfortable around him.

- **Teach your child how to rescue himself from an odd situation:** Talk with your child about dangerous or odd situations that might arise before him/her. Ask your 14- year-old daughter what she would do if a guest arrived at a party with a bottle of wine in her overnight bag. Ask your 12-year-old son how he would handle a suggestion from a friend to cut school and head for a nearby burger place.

  Preferably, youngsters themselves will not allow to prevail an imminently dangerous or destructive situation. However, if they are yet to learn this skill, parent Maria Joseph from Cochin suggests an alternative: "Sometimes kids don't want to do what their peers want them to do. I tell my kids to blame me — to tell their friends that their Mom says 'no'. This helps get them off the hook." Ultimately, no child going out for an evening should be without change for a phone call. As a last resort, this may be his lifeline. A cell phone may also be an apt choice if the family can afford one and if the child knows how to use the phone responsibly.

- **Keep a check on friendships to help your child evade harmful behaviour:** Even after school hours, young adolescents need supervision and guidance. Just monitor who your child's friends are and what they do when they assemble. Brijesh Chauhan, a middle school teacher in Mumbai, urges, "Don't be afraid to be the jerk that makes the phone call to the other house to make sure that (your child) is there. And don't be afraid to say no."

A number of middle school teachers and parents differ in their opinions whether parents can or should try to stop their children from meeting a friend that the parents dislike. Some youngsters will rebel if they are told so. Many adults who have spent quality time with young teens suggest that you let your child know that you disapprove of a friendship and why you disapprove. They also suggest to limit the amount of time and the activities that parents allow with the friend.

- **Exemplify good friendships:** The friendship you exemplify leave a deep impact on your child's friendships than any lecture. Children who find their parents treat each other and their friends with politeness and affection have an advantage. Baking cookies for the new neighbour or offering a listening ear for an annoyed friend sends your child a strong message.

Many adults who have spent quality time with young teens suggest that you let your child know that you disapprove of a friendship and why you disapprove.

x x x

"If you are a parent, open doors to unknown directions to the child so he can explore. Don't make him afraid of the unknown, give his support."
~Osho

MEDIA

"I am always trying to evolve, so I like to read
parenting books and things like that."
~Kourtney Kardashian

What should I do to keep away the media's bad Impact upon my child?

It's not easy to understand the world of early adolescents without viewing the deepening impact of mass media on their lives. It competes with families, friends, schools and communities in its ability to mould the interests, attitudes and worth of young teens.

Their lives are infiltrated by mass media. Most young adolescents watch TV and movies, surf the Internet, exchange e-mails, and listen to CDs and to radio stations that target them with music and commercials and read articles and ads in cult magazines published especially for teens.

At the outset, have an optimistic view. The children use new media technologies as fun and excitement. Used wisely, they can also educate themselves; that's why entertainment at many places has been replaced with edutainment. Good TV programs can be informative in its steak, good music can sooth the ears and good movies can expand interests and unlock mysteries. Moreover, many forms of media are being used in classrooms today — computers, cable-equipped TVs and DVDs are all part of the landscape. Of course, today classrooms in many schools are being connected to the Internet and provided a reasonable number of computers to each classroom for student use. Resultantly, children need to be exposed to media, if only to learn how to use it.

The obstacles in the way is that young adolescents often don't — or can't — distinguish between what's good in the media and what's bad. Some spend hours watching the TV or plugged into earphones, passively taking in what they see and hear— violence, sex, profanities, stereotyping and storylines and characters that are impracticable. We know from such research as conducted by Gopal Kumar and Ambika Shekhar that seeing too much TV violence appears to increase aggressive behaviour in children and that regular viewing of violence makes violence less shocking and more acceptable.

Students who keep themselves adhered to TV most of the time, have lower grades and lower test scores than do those who watch less TV. "In any classroom discussion I have, it is very apparent who's watching [too much] television and who's not," explains teacher Neha Kumar. "For the kids who are not motivated in the classroom, mention TV and suddenly they perk up."

With growing maturity in young teens, watching TV, playing video-game, using computer and surfing of Internet increase accordingly. On average, Indian children spend far more time with the media than they devote their time to school assignments. Comparatively, seventh graders, for example, spend an average of 135 minutes each day watching TV and 57 minutes doing school assignment.

According to the recent reports by the Indian Government, the number of overweight teens in India has increased surprisingly over the past two decades. Being overweight, in turn, can contribute to serious health repercussions, such as diabetes and other related ailments.

Other media also remain on the forefront to exert negative influences. For example, a growing number of ads in magazines, including some for harmful products such as alcohol and tobacco, are preying young adolescents.

Your will benefit your child in helping him to balance media-related activities with other activities such as reading, talking with family and spending time with friends. Here are some ways that you can help your child make good media choices:

- **Determine a limit of time your child spends on watching TV:** Indeed, it's nearly impossible to protect your child entirely from the media. However, absolute prohibition of viewing TV may only strengthen its appeal to her. Though some parents do make TV viewing off-limits during the school week, except for special programs that are agreed to ahead of time, yet children remain unable to resist the fascination.

  It must be kept in mind that it's not hard to restrict your child's poor media choices if you say no before she brings home the objectionable CDs or computer games or turns on the violent TV programs. Let your child know that you will monitor her media choices.

- **Have a check on what your child watches and listens to:** Former principal Ritu Chandra advises, "Don't just listen to how loud the music is, but to what the words are." Learn about the TV programs and movies that your child wants to watch, the computer games he wants to play and the music he wants to listen to. Knowing something about your child's interests will let you enter into his world and talk with more knowledge and force about his choices. Ask your young teen what bands or singers he likes.

Then read about his favourites in magazines or newspapers or listen to their CDs or to the radio stations that play their music.

- **Parents can also watch or listen *with* their child:** This allows you to spend time with him and to learn more about the programs, games and music that he likes. Talk with your child about what you are seeing and hearing.

- **Suggest TV programs that you consider your child to watch:** Encourage your child to watch TV programs about a variety of subjects — nature, travel, history, science, biography and news, as well as programs that entertain. News and history programs, for example, can encourage discussions about world issues, national and local politics, social problems and health concerns.

- **Negotiate with your child on the difference between facts and opinions:** There is need to infuse in teens' minds that not everything they hear or see is true. Let your child know that the TV show or movie he watches, the radio station or music he listens to and the magazine he reads may have a definite opinion. Talk with him about how the media can promote certain ideas or beliefs, which may differ from those of your family. If your child wants to watch, listen to or read something that you believe is inappropriate, let him know exactly why you object.

- **Discuss with your child on misleading ads:** Young adolescents are especially susceptible to fascinating advertising. Talk with your child about what ads are for — to sell products — and about how to judge whether the products the ads sell are right for him. If, for example, your daughter has short, blond, curly hair, ask her if she really thinks the shampoo that she wants you to spend Rs. 50 for will make her hair look like the long, black, straight hair on the model in the magazine ad.

- **Prioritise buying a TV with a child lock facility:** A child lock facility can block your child from watching pornographic, violent or other indecent TV channels.

- **Discuss with your child on the risks of visiting computer chat rooms:** Let your child know the perils of "talking" online with strangers. There is software that can restrict children from chat rooms, even as they allow access to other content.

- **Discuss with other parents:** Taking on movies, TV shows, computer games and CDs with the parents of your child's friends and classmates can give you more strength to say *no* when he wants to see or hear something that think is inappropriate. You also can quickly find out that *not everyone* in the seventh grade is going to be allowed to see the latest R-rated movie in which bloody bodies are strewn across the screen.

- **Provide substitute of media entertainment:** Brijesh Chauhan, a teacher by profession, says, "If you give the kids enough activities, the TV goes away." Given the opportunity, many children would rather *do* than *watch*. A day at a miniature golf course or a visit with a friend may hold more appeal for your child than watching TV.

- **Model substitute of entertainment:** If parents constantly watch TV or anything on YouTube, their young teen would use this opportunity to play games on mobile or check his/her mail and so on. But when the same parents turn off the TV or computer and engage in conversation, sports, games or other activities with their teen, they show substitutes to him/her.

Generally, Indian children spend more time on media than doing their school assignments.

✗ ✗ ✗

HAPPINESS IS WHEN...

YOU REALIZE YOUR CHILDREN HAVE TURNED OUT TO BE GOOD PEOPLE.

THE MIDDLE GRADES

"Parenthood remains the greatest single preserve of
the amateur."
~Alvin Toffler

What Is school like for young adolescents?

You might have definitely attended a primary school. It
possibly combined grades seven through nine and has a
replica of high school. You probably moved from class to
class throughout the school day and had different
teachers for different subjects.

For the past two decades, many changes have taken
place in how young adolescents are being educated. These
changes are perennial as we learn more about how these
children develop and learn. Today, fewer and fewer
young adolescents attend primary school. Instead, a
growing number attend middle schools. Most of these

schools are for grades VI-VIII, albeit some may have grades V-VIII, V-VII or even VII-VIII. As the middle school movement has picked up its pace, many high schools have moved from serving grades X-XII to grades IX-XII.

Most educators believe (and research confirms) that the way a school organises the grades is not as crucial as what happens inside the school. That is, *what* gets taught and *how* it gets taught in a school matter more than how the school combines its grades. Moreover, the grade span of a school doesn't acquaint you much with the standard of the school and whether its educational practices appropriately suits to young adolescent students.

The majority of young teens taking admission in a new school find that it's a big change. They're used to being the oldest; once again they're the youngest. Many classmates are new, as are the routines and the school assignment. Coming at a time when young teens are undergoing various other stressful changes, the move to a new school can be overwhelming and have a negative impact on motivation and self-honour.

Due to this, many middle schools have made programs to transition relatively easier. For example, they might invite elementary school students to visit the middle school to become familiar with the building, lockers and changing classrooms. Or, administrators of the middle and elementary schools might call a meeting to discuss the programs. School counsellors might meet to talk about how to help students make a smooth transition. These practices can help them make the new school environment more amicable.

Though there may be consistency in fluctuation of hormones, young teens of all backgrounds and with a broad spectrum of personal qualities still obtain vast amounts of information. They can also benefit from a strong curriculum. As young adolescents develop their cognitive skills, they are able to accomplish longer and more involved projects and to explore subjects by diving deeper than earlier.

Generally, young teens get benefited by their exposure to a broad range of experiences and programs based on academic, recreational and vocational streams. These opportunities take advantage of their natural aspiration and can be invaluable in familiarising them with new worlds and possibilities. These exploratory programs can also be fun for them. Considering these aspects, some schools provide opportunities both in and out of school for students to ease their participation in sports, as well as in programs to teach subjects ranging from foreign languages, to music, drama, technology and so on. Many schools also encourage students to participate voluntarily in social and community service projects. Exploratory programs can help young teens figure out where they fit in and allow them to think about their future plans.

Still, there is plenteous room for improvement in middle schools. Test scores suggest that many young teens lack the skills required for high school success. When compared internationally, they aren't scoring as satisfactorily as we would like in areas such as reading and math.

There are an increasing number of educators and policy-makers who are becoming aware of the high levels to which young teens can achieve. This awareness is leading to still more change in middle-grades education: in what gets taught, how it is taught, how teachers are prepared and how to assess what students know and can perform in their life.

Exploratory programs can help young teens figure out where they fit in and allow them to think about their future plans.

✗ ✗ ✗

Happiness is when...

you realize your children have turned out to be good people.

PARENTS' PARTICIPATION

"Parenting now is a two-way relationship where you learn from each other."
~ *Juhi Chawla*

How can the parents participate in their child's school activities?

It is said that a child never gets old in the eyes of his/her parents, and that's why he/she always needs your guidance almost in every initiative of your life. Your young teen needs you throughout his life more than he may admit (to you or to himself) — although he may want you present under different terms and conditions than he did earlier. Some parents misread the signals that their children send and back off too soon. For example, for children at age nine, about 75 per cent of Indian parents report high or moderate participation in school-related activities, but when children attain the age of 14, the rate of parents' involvement declines to 55 per cent. The rate continues to decline throughout high school.

According to research, adolescents do better in school when their parents get involved in their lives and that education works best when teachers and parents work together sharing their wisdom and experiences with one another. Here are some tips for staying involved in your child's school life:

- **Set basic rules for your child at the beginning of the school year:** Since the first day of school, ensure that your child knows what time he is expected to sleep and wake up, what he needs to do to get ready for school each morning and what time he needs to leave home for school. Check that he knows his curfew both on weekdays and on the weekend. Also make sure that your child knows that he is expected to try vigorously and excel in school.

- **Familiarise yourself with your child's school:** The more you know, the easier your task will be as parent. Ask for a school handbook. This will clear your many queries that will arise over the year. If your school doesn't have a handbook, prepare questions to be answered. Ask the principal and teachers, for example: What classes does the school offer? Which classes are required? What are your expectations from my child? How does the school evaluate the students' progress? What are the school's rules and regulations?

- **Know about the school's homework policy:**
  Knowing school policies for homework merits vital importance because by the middle grades, homework generally plays a major role in your child's grades and test scores than it did in elementary school. Try to know from teachers how often they will home assignments and about how long they may take to complete.

  Do *not* do your child's homework. However, make sure that he tries his best to complete it.

- **Help your child get organised:** Many young teens easily deviate from the right track. With so much to do and think about, it's not astonishing. The amount of their school work and their extracurricular activities often get enhanced at the same time that they are going through a growth spurt, developing new relationship and trying to develop more independence. Young teens respond to these changes in different ways, but a number of them daydream, forget things, lose things and seem ignorant of time. It's not unusual for a middle schooler to accomplish his home assignment but forget to turn it in. Some schools help students develop organisational skills. Others leave the task to you. Whatever the case, you can:

- Go over your child's schedule together to see if he's/she's got too much of tasks at once. Discuss with him on setting priorities and dropping certain activities if necessary or rearranging the routine of some of them.

- Help him develop good study habits. Let him set a routine for him to do homework regularly. Talk about the assignments. Make sure he understands and is able to do what he/ she's supposed to do. Make sure he has a calendar to record assignments, as well as a backpack and homework folders in which to tuck assignments for safekeeping.

- Help your child get started when he has to do research reports or other major assignments, perhaps by taking him to the library or helping him find the sources of online information from appropriate Web sites.

- Urge your child to avoid last-minute cramming by working out a schedule of what he needs to do to prepare for the test.

- Work alongside your child to clean out his backpack or clean up his room.

• **Create an environment at home that encourages learning and school activities:**

Provide a quiet time without TV and other distractions when homework assignments can be completed. If you live in a small or noisy household, try having all family members participate in a quiet activity during homework time. You may need to take a noisy toddler outside or into another room to play and it will work well if you do so by alluring him by offering some sweets or toys etc. If distractions couldn't be avoided, you may help your child complete assignments in the local library.

Let your child know that you value education. Show him that the skills he is learning are an important part of the things he will do as an adult. Let him see you reading books, newspapers and computer screens; writing reports, letters, e-mails and lists; using math to balance your checkbook or to measure for new carpeting; and doing things that require thought and effort. Tell your child about what you do at work.

Show him that the skills he is learning are an important part of the things he will do as an adult.

- **Attend school events:** Attend sports events and concerts, back-to-school night, PTA meetings and awards events, such as a "perfect attendance" breakfast. Always keep in mind, though many young teens are often self-conscious and want parents' presence beside them but in the background. "They want you there, but they want you at more of a distance," explains teacher Brijesh Chauhan. Look for school activities that you can do with your child like cleaning up the school grounds, decorating classrooms and so on.

- **Volunteer in your child's school:** If your schedule allows, look for ways to help out at your child's school. Schools often send home lists of ways how parents can get themselves involved. Chaperones are needed for school trips or dances. School committees need members and the school newsletter may need an editor to refine the requisite matters to be published. The school may have councils or advisory committees that seek parent representatives. If work or other commitments make it impossible for you to volunteer in the school, look for ways to help at home itself. For example, you can make phone calls to other parents to tell them about school-related activities.

- **Keep in touch with the school, teachers and school authorities:** Keeping in touch can be a bit difficult if your child has many teachers, but at the very least it's good to know your child's counsellor and a favourite teacher. The more noticeable you are, the more educators will be able to communicate openly and regularly with you. Attend parent-teacher meetings/ conferences. Read school bulletins when they are sent home. You can suggest the school authorities something beneficial if you find so after going through the bulletins.

- **Make sure the classes your child attends will enable him to attend college:** Middle school or junior school is by no means too early to plan for your child's future. A three or four year college degree is becoming more and more important for finding a good job. Collegeswant studentsand employerswant workers who have taken certain professional/technical courses and acquired a solid base of skills and knowledge. Good courses for college-bound students include English, science (biology, chemistry, earth science and physics), history or geography, besides algebra and geometry. Many colleges also require applicants to study a foreign language for at least two years and some prefer three or four years of one language course. Basic computer skills are also essential and many colleges view participation in the arts and music as valuable and job-oriented also.

- **Monitor how well your child is doing in school:** Report cards tell you about the performance of your child. But you also need to know how things are going between report cards. For example, if your son/daughter is having trouble in math, find out when he has his next math test and when it will be returned to him. This allows you to address a problem before it mushrooms into something bigger. Contact the teacher if your child doesn't understand an assignment or if he needs extra help to complete an assignment.

The more noticeable you are, the more educators will be able to communicate openly and regularly with you.

✗ ✗ ✗

There is no job more IMPORTANT *than* **parenting**. *This I believe.*

~Ben Carson

READING

"What can you do to promote world peace? Go home
and love your family."
~*Mother Teresa*

How should I help my child become a successful reader?

It's during the middle grades when young adolescents
build the foundation for lifelong reading habits. They
develop their own reading interests and learn to read
different kinds of reading materials. They increase their
vocabularies by reading widely and start utilising reading
to help answer important questions about themselves and
the world.

However, for many young adolescents, reading difficulties persist with social and emotional problems.

So, it is vitally important for you to keep your child reading throughout the adolescent years, both at school and home. Here are some suggestions that can help:

- **Make sure your home abounds in useful reading materials:** It's not necessary that only expensive books and magazines will be good and worth reading. You can often find decent and useful reading materials for your child at yard, weekly book hatt, or library sales. Take initiative in giving your child as well as other children books and magazine subscriptions as gifts for birthdays or other special occasions and ask your family members and friends to carry on this initiative. Fix a quiet time for family reading. Some families even enjoy reading aloud to each other, with each family member choosing a book, story, poem or article to read to the others.

- **Encourage your child to use the library:** Take your child to the local library and help him get his own library card. Ask librarians to help him locate different areas in the library, use the card catalogue or computer system and find materials of his interest.

- **Be a positive role model for reading:** Let your child watch you enjoy reading as well as performing your routine activities as an adult —

reading letters and recipes, directions and instructions, newspapers, computer screens and so forth. Go with him to the library and check out books for yourself. When your child sees that reading is important to you, he may decide that it's important to him, too.

- **Learn from your child's teachers how they encourage or teach reading:** Make it clear that you value reading as a fructuous habit and that you support homework assignments that require your child to read. Ask for the lists of books for your child to read independently at home.

- **Learn how to help your child if his first language is not English:** After getting your child admitted in middle school, talk with his teachers, who generally, welcome such talks. If you need some support in getting access to the teachers, take help of a relative, neighbour or someone else in your acquaintance to go with you. When you meet, tell the teachers the things you are doing at home to strengthen your child's reading habit. Children who can switch back and forth between languages have accomplished something special. They should be praised and encouraged as they work for this achievement.

- **Help your child tackle the problem if he has a reading problem:** If a child has reading difficulties, the reason might be simple to understand and deal with. For example, your child might have trouble seeing and needs glasses or he may just need more help with reading skills. If you think that your child needs extra help, ask teachers about special services that may prove effective in overcoming the difficulties. Also ask teachers or your local librarian for names of community organisations and local literacy volunteer groups that offer tutoring services.

Some causes for reading difficulties signal larger problems, perhaps a learning disability. If you think your child may have some kind of physical or learning problem that needs to be solved medically, it is crucial to consult an expert specialised for the same. Ask for a private meeting with his counsellor, a teacher or the principal.

There is a law — the Right to Education — that may allow you to get certain services for your child from your school zone. Your child might qualify to get help from a reading specialist, a speech and language therapist or other specialist. You can learn about your special education rights and responsibilities by requesting that the school give you — in your first language — a summary of legal rights.

Ask teachers or your local librarian for names of community organisations and local literacy volunteer groups that offer tutoring services.

✗ ✗ ✗

EVERY
CHILD IS A
different KIND OF flower,
AND ALL TOGETHER,
MAKE THIS WORLD
A Beautiful
GARDEN.

MOTIVATION

"At the end of the day, the most overwhelming key to
a child's success is the positive involvement of
parents."
~*Jane D. Hull*

How should I keep my child motivated to learn and do well, both in and out of school?

Psychologist Bhawna Diwaker defines motivation as "the love of learning, the love of challenge." In her opinion, motivation is often more important than initial ability in determining our success.

Yet somewhere in the middle grades the motivation of some young adolescents for learning takes a nosedive. A young teen may begin to grumble about assignments and teachers, ask to drop out of a favourite activity, complain that he/she's bored or show signs of being lost in the educational shuffle.

Here are some of the things that can cause low motivation:

- **Biological changes:** The onset of puberty—getting her period or being 4 feet 2 inches tall when your buddy is 5 feet 10 inches — distracts some teens. Distractions make it hard to think about the swim team or the social studies project that's due.

- **Emotional concerns:** It may require extra effort to concentrate on a science project when he is preoccupied with physical insecurities or concerned about being excluded from a special group.

- **The school environment:** There is possibility that a young teen may lose motivation after moving from elementary school to a middle school or junior school. The loss of motivation can be fuelled by insufficient support in the new school or by an increased workload and expectations to which the student hasn't yet adjusted.

- **Social and peer pressures:** Social and peer pressures have two sides of one coin. Such pressures either force a child to put more hard work to excel or he may fall victim to despondency. Here also, parents can play an effective role to encourage their child to work harder in comparison to his peers. If he is compared with the performance of a girl peer, he would try more vigorously to excel in his objectives.

- **A move in how your child views his ability:** Younger children tend to believe that the harder you try, the smarter you'll become. But Dr. Bhawna Diwaker remarks that as children move into their early teens, they may start believing that ability is fixed and to compare their ability with that of others — the harder you *have* to try, the less able you *must* be. This view can dampen your child's motivation. Why try hard if it won't help you to do well?

- **Lack of opportunities:** Non-affordability often becomes the reason behind lack of opportunities, due to which, some youngsters remain unable to take the classes or participate in the activities that they need to fuel their enthusiasm. This is most likely with students from disadvantaged families or who are at risk, contributing to perceptions that they remain to be unmotivated.

- **Preferring short-cut solution:** On the basis of their observation, some educators report that it's hard to get students to focus on a long history project when they're used to TV programs and media presentations that are fast, short and entertaining also.

The loss of motivation can be fuelled by insufficient support in the new school or by an increased workload and expectations to which the student hasn't yet adjusted.

- **Immature work ethic:** Some unmotivated youngsters may not have learned that making success in school requires more time and efforts. Many attractions compete for students' attention and, according to some research; some students expect school and activities to be consistently exciting and pleasant. They aren't aware of the fact that both in school and daily life, they can learn valuable lessons from such activities that aren't always fun and that achievement usually requires real effort. You can encourage and create opportunities for your child, but ultimately your son is responsible for seeing that his homework gets done and your daughter must be the one to practice the dance.

Here are the ways to enhance your child's motivation:

- **Be an ideal role model:** Young teens benefit from watching their parents putting forth their best effort, completing work and meeting obligations. Parents need to demonstrate that they value learning and hard work for the desired success.

- **Convince your child to believe that sustained effort over time is the key to achievement:** Teach him to set high goals and to work much harder to achieve them. Help him to see the value of tackling the challenges and of finding ways to meet or exceed those challenges.

- **Steer your child towards appropriate classes and suitable activities:** Young teens need opportunities to excel and be an asset for their parents, family, society and nation. Success can be a powerful motivator and boredom may be a sign that your child hasn't enough opportunities to develop his talents. He may need an advanced English class, an art class or the chance to volunteer at a homeless shelter.

- **Extend your support:** Boosting and praise without reasons or praise for poor efforts is no help, but young teens need to be reassured that they can do something. "Sometimes kids will say they are bored or have developed monotony, but it's because they haven't done it [an activity] before," advises teacher Babita Shah. Your child may need hints about how to get started with a new project from you, another adult, an instructor or a book.

- **Gain strengths and build on them:** Every child has potential to shine in some area. Identify what your child's forte is and what he can do best, no matter what it is.

- **When necessary, consult your child's teachers, counsellors or school principal:** A drop in grades is not uncommon and should not be made a factor of discouragement when students go from one grade level to another. But if your child's grade drop is extreme or persists for more than one marking period, contact someone at the school. It's OK to be a strong but respectful advocate for your child. Because middle-grades teachers may have very full schedules, you may need to show persistence. Get in touch with the teachers if you find many assignments inappropriate or if your child is unable to accomplish them. Take the lead if your child is placed in classes that you think are poor in content or that fails to provide your child the sufficient stimuli.

- **Have realistic expectations:** It's important to hold children to high esteem. But when young teens are asked to do something impossible, they may recede from taking initiative in this way. Don't pressurise your 5-foot 4-inch son/daughter to try out for centre on his/her basketball team just because he/she played centre for his elementary school team. Instead, reassure him/

her that, in time, he/she'll grow taller and help him/her to look for other activities in the meantime. Having realistic expectations also requires you to consider your child's ability, personality and temperament. Your 6-foot son/daughter may not enjoy playing basketball. Make sure that your child knows, deep in his heart, that you love him for what he *is* and not for what he *does.*

- **Keep patience:** Children's motivation starts improving gradually if parents take the above-given steps. However, keeping patience is a must for parents: Many young teens need the gift of time to develop the maturity that allows them to complete homework assignments and chores with preferably least supervision.

Make sure that your child knows, deep in his heart, that you love him for what he is and not for what he does.

x x x

"The voice of parents is the voice of gods, for to their children they are heaven's lieutenants."   ~William Shakespeare

VALUES

"The moment a child is born, the mother is also born.
She never existed before."
-Osho

What should I do to help my child develop appreciable values and learn to distinguish right from wrong?

We want our children to develop respect and compassion for others. We want them to be honest, decent and thoughtful — to stand up for their principles, to cooperate with others and to act responsibly. We want them to make sound moral choices. The pay-offs for encouraging a child's values are enormous: those who grow up with strong, consistent and positive values are happier, do better in school and are more likely to contribute to society and nation.

Discuss with your children good values and why they matter in life

Just as children need to be guided academically, so too must they be educated in the values of a civil society — values like cherishing love for your neighbour; paying honestly justified wages for an honest day's work; telling the truth and be steadfast in honesty; respecting others; and taking responsibility for your decisions.

Whether it is verbal or practical, parents play an important role in helping their children develop a good sense of distinguishing right from wrong and good from bad.

Most of the major threats to our children today are not a matter of chance, but a matter of choice — choices like drinking and driving, smoking, drugs, sex, and dropping out of school suffice to spoil their career and even life.

According to research, young people who engage themselves in one risky behaviour are more likely to participate in others, so parents should help their children understand the potential risks and consequences of their choices —not just for the immediate future but for their lifetime also.

Fortunately, most children share the values of their parents about the most important things. Your priorities and principles and your example of good behaviour can teach young teens to replicate you, thereby taking the high road when other roads look tempting. Here are some ways that you can help your child develop good values:

- If you stick with a challenging job, your child will be more inclined to finish homework and chores.

- When you say "no" to alcohol before heading out on the highway, your child takes note.

- When you accept a loss on the basketball court graciously, your child can learn that winning isn't everything.

- If your child finds his parents treating each other with respect, he is more likely to follow this example in dating and into marriage.

- When your son/daughter senses that his parents appreciate people of all colours and creeds, he is likely to become more open to friends of all races and backgrounds.

- When you tell a sales clerk that he gave you change for a hundred-rupee bill and not a fifty, your child sees honesty in action.

- When your child see his parents make tough choices — "We're buying a used car so that we can save more money for a vacation" — he picks up the cues and learns how to save money and be austere.

- If you accept disappointments as a part of life — if you pick yourself up and keep going — your child stands a better chance of becoming a survivor.

- If you can laugh at your own mistakes, your child is more likely to accept his own imperfections. This laugh will pave his way for making attempts for perfection.

- When you volunteer at a food kitchen, your child will be more likely to have compassion for others who are less fortunate.

Your priorities and principles and your example of good behaviour can teach young teens to take the high road when other roads look tempting.

The way that you view money and material goods can also mould your child's attitudes. If you see your self-worth and the worth of others in terms of cars, homes, furniture, nice clothes and other possessions, your child is more likely to develop these attitudes as well. It is equally important to meet your child's *needs* but to guide him to set them apart from his *wants*. The expensive leather jacket that he *has to have* may be OK — but it is subject to your affordability.

Giving your child an allowance is one good way to help her/him understand the value of money. But you must decide the amount of allowance he exactly deserves, taking into account your resources, your child's age and what expenses the allowance will cover (lunches, clothes, church donations, entertainment or whatever). An allowance can help your young teen learn how to save and how to use money wisely.

It's but natural for parents to disclose information and provide guidance that is consistent with their values and religious beliefs. We know from child development experts that parents are often better at providing information about the facts of life than they are at talking about what matters more: their values concerning sexuality. To make good decisions, young teens need to have accurate information about "the birds and the bees" that takes into consideration strong values.

Parents often find it easier to teach their children values when they rely on their friends and other parents for support and guidance. Many parents also draw support from their churches, synagogues, mosques or other religious institutions.

At some point in their adolescent-rearing efforts, many parents find themselves disappointed and frustrated. ("I can't believe my kid did something so dumb and insensitive. What did I do wrong?") Generally, there is no reason to panic if your child sometimes behaves in a way that differs from your standards — as long as he doesn't do it regularly. Bad behaviour needs to be recognised and dealt with appropriately. But we would all do well to remember our own adolescence — most of us turned out OK.

An allowance can help your young teen learn how to save and how to use money wisely.

$$\times \times \times$$

The best security blanket a child can have is parents who respect each others.

-Jane Blaustone

PROBLEMS

"My children are the reason I laugh, smile and want to
get up every morning."
~*Gena Lee Nolin*

What should I do – If my child is facing a serious problem?

Most youngsters from the age group of 10 to 14 are not as troubled as their stereotype suggests. They manage the bumps of adolescence successfully. Still, you need to be a ubiquitous guard for him. According to one study, 28 per cent of India's eighth-graders have experimented with alcohol/drugs, although a much smaller percentage goes on to develop serious alcohol/drug problems. Some young teens develop eating disorders. Others suffer from depression and other emotional problems. In some cases, emotional problems are linked to learning disabilities that have not been diagnosed or treated.

Some factors that can place a young teen at greater risk for developing problems include:

- growing up in poverty;

- living in a single-parent home;

- being male;

- growing up in a neighbourhood lacking social supports;

- lacking adequate supervision from his/her elders;

- having poor relationships with their parents or other adults who are important to them;

- having low self-esteem;

- attending poor-quality schools; or

- experiencing physical abuse, sexual abuse or neglect.

Don't assume that being "at-risk" automatically means trouble for a child. Some young teens with many risk factors escape major problems, while some with fewer risk factors stagger .

We know that certain things enable the children to escape major problems. Having warm, supportive parents who also draw clear rules and monitor sufficiently is key. In addition, a child with an easy-going temperament, good socio-communication skills and a good sense of humour is generally able to deal with problems. A child who attends school and lives in neighbourhood that provides many supports is also, on average, more able to bounce back from trouble. These supports include people who take a special interest in them — for example, teachers, coaches or neighbours.

Though this book is cannot address each and every problem at length like a panacea, yet it is like a caveat. It helps to recognise the warning signs for some major problems and the resources section lists materials organisations, Web sites and hotlines that can provide you with further direction and help.

One warning: You may have to address more than one problem at the same time, because serious problems are likely appear together in one child: a 12-year-old with an eating disorder may also be a victim of depression, while a 14-year-old who uses alcohol/tobacco may also be sexually active.

You may have to address more than one problem at the same time, because serious problems are likely appear together in one child.

Alcohol or Tobacco Addiction

Since early adolescence can be a period of confusion and stress for children, it is not surprising that this is the period when many of them first try to have the taste of alcohol, tobacco and other drugs.

Since mood swings and unpredictable behaviour are common among young teens, parents often find it hard to spot the signs of alcohol and drug abuse. If your child starts showing some of the following signs, tobacco or alcohol may be at the heart of the problem:

- He's withdrawn, depressed, tired and careless about personal grooming.

- She's hostile and uncooperative and often breaks curfews.

- He has new friends (and may not want to talk about them).

- He doesn't want to reveal you where he is going and what he is going to do.

- His grades slip.

- He/she's lost interest in hobbies, sports and other activities that were once favourites.

- He experiences change in his eating or sleeping patterns; indulging in adverse sleeping habit as he/she's up late at night and sleeps during the day.

- His relationship with family members has worsened and he refuses to discuss school, activities, friends or other important subjects that pertain to his career-building.

- He has trouble concentrating and seems forgetful.

- His eyes are red-rimmed and/or his nose is runny despite catching no cold.

- Household money keeps disappearing.

Eating Disorders

Eating orders usually occur in females. Eating disorders in males are usually associated with athletics, especially wrestling. Since wrestlers need more energy to wrestle, they indulge in overeating and wrong choice of food.

The most common eating disorders are *anorexia nervosa* and *bulimia*. Anorexia is an emotional disorder that can be signalled by severe weight loss or failure to gain weight. About 90 per cent of the people who have this disorder are females. Studies suggest that one in 250 young women may suffer from anorexia, with symptoms most often first appearing in early to middle adolescence. Bulimia can be signalled by episodes of binge eating followed by self- induced vomiting, fasting or strenuous exercise. Bulimia tends to develop among older adolescents, many of whom have also been anorexic.

Many physical disorders such as kidney problems, irregular heart rhythms, irritation and tears in the esophagus, dizziness or fainting and stomach and intestinal problems are associated with eating disorders. The death rate is from 5 to 15 per cent, but it is lower if sufferers receive timely and appropriate treatment.

Take your worries to an expert if your child:

- loses a large amount of weight for no medical reason;

- reduces the amount of food he eats and/or stops eating high carbohydrate and fatty foods;

- exercises excessively despite weakness and fatigue;

- possesses an intense fear of gaining weight;

- stops menstruating;

- binges on foods that are high in calories; or

- tries to control her weight by vomiting or using laxatives or diuretics.

Depression and Suicide

An increase in suicides among young adolescents makes it vital for parents to recognise the causes and symptoms.

Many factors can contribute to serious depression leading to commitment of suicide. If a parent suffers from extreme depression, a child is more likely to experience it too. But circumstances such as broken or unhappy families, the bereavement of parent through divorce or death, sexual abuse or drug or alcohol abuse may also contribute to depression. Other stressful situations may also play a role: for example, losing a relative, being ignored by friends or serious concerns about sexuality.

Some warning signs of depression and possible suicidal tendencies include:

- Change in sleeping patterns (either sleeping too much or too little);

- Change in behaviour (can't concentrate on school, work or routine tasks, slipping grades);

- Change in personality (seems sad, withdrawn, irritable, anxious, tired, indecisive, apathetic);

- Change in eating habits (loss of appetite and weight or overeating);

- Physical changes, (including a lack of energy, sudden weight gain or loss, lack of interest in appearance);

- A major loss or life change (through death, divorce, separation, broken relationship);

- Decreased interest in friends, school or activities;

- Low self-esteem (feeling worthless, overwhelming guilt, self-hatred);

- No hope for the future (believes things will never get better, that nothing will ever change);

- Preoccupation with music, art and personal writing about death;

- Giving away prized possessions and otherwise "getting affairs in order;" and

- Direct suicide threats or comments such as, "I wish I was dead!" "My family would be better off without me." or "I don't have anything to live for." These threats should always be taken seriously and the remedial measures must be taken soon.

Learning Disabilities

The Ministry of Health estimates that 15 per cent of the Indian population has some type of learning disability. Learning-disabled students have a neurological disorder that creates difficulty in how they store, use or produce information. They are as intelligent as anyone else and they often perform very well in art, music or sports. But a gap may exist between their ability and their performance and thus, they may have trouble with reading, writing, speaking or mathematics, and even with social relationships. Most often, learning-disabled students need to work harder to make up for their learning problems. This can leave them open to depression and reduce confidence, particularly if the disability goes untreated.

Look for these warning signs of learning disabilities. One or two of these signs in your child will not be the reason for concern, but the presence of several can signal the caution for help:

- Often reverses letters in writing, such as writing *felt* for *left*.

- Has trouble learning spelling strategies, such as using information from prefixes, suffixes and root words.

- Avoids reading aloud.

- Avoids writing compositions.

- Has trouble with handwriting or avoids it altogether.

- Holds a pencil awkwardly.

- Has trouble recalling facts.

Attention Deficit Disorder (ADD) or ADHD (which includes hyperactivity), is not a learning disability, although about one fifth of ADD students have learning disabilities. These students are distracted so easily and have a hard time staying focused.

If you believe your young teen has a learning disability, consult your paediatrician, your child's teachers and the school counsellor, who can guide you to find the exact solution.

Most often, learning-disabled students must need to work harder to make up for their learning deficiencies.

ⅩⅩⅩ

Having a baby is a life-changer. It gives you a whole other perspective on why you wake up every day.

~Taylor Hanson

CONCLUSION

"It is easier to build strong children than to repair
broken men."
~*Frederick Douglass*

No one can guarantee that young adolescents will grow into responsible and competent adults. Learning well about the world of early adolescents is an important step towards helping your child— and you — through the fascinating, confusing and wonderful years from 10 through 14. As a middle school teacher, Suresh Jindal from Delhi puts it, early adolescence is "never dull, never boring." Stay tuned to the life of your young teen and enjoy this special time.

✗ ✗ ✗

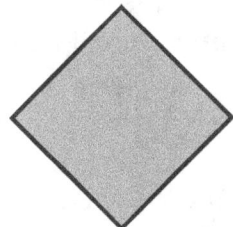

OVERVIEW OF ADOLESCENTS

"Let us Sacrifice our Today so that our Children can have Better Tomorrow."
~*APJ Abdul Kalam*

Loosely defined as the years between 11 and 19, adolescence is considered a critical phase of development– and not just in outward appearances.

"The brain continues to change throughout life, but there are huge leaps in development during adolescence," explains Sara Johnson, an assistant professor at the Johns Hopkins Bloomberg School of Public Health.

And just as a teen may go through an awkward growth spurt, new cognitive skills and competencies may come in leaps and stutters. Parents should understand that no matter how tall their son has sprouted or how grown-up their daughter dresses, "they are still in a developmental period that will affect the rest of their life."

With the course of growth in brain, the teen brain becomes more interconnected and gains processing power. Adolescents start to have the computational and decision-making skills like an adult –if given time and access to information.

"But in the heat of the moment, their decision-making can be overly influenced by emotions, because their brains rely more on the limbic system (the emotional seat of the brain) than the more rational prefrontal cortex," explained Feinstein.

"This duality of adolescent competence can be very confusing for parents," Johnson said, meaning that sometimes teens do things, like punch a wall or drive too fast, when, if asked, they clearly know better.

Scientists used to think only infants have an overabundance of neuronal connections, which are "pruned" into a more efficient arrangement over the first three years of life.

But it has been discovered that a second burst of neuronal sprouting occurs right before puberty, peaking at about age 11 for girls and 12 for boys.

The adolescent's experiences – from reading vampire novels to learning to drive – shape this new grey matter, mostly following a "use it or lose it" strategy, Johnson said. The structural reorganization is thought to continue until the age of 25, and smaller changes continue throughout life.

Adolescents are in the midst of acquiring incredible new skills sets, especially when it comes to social behaviour and abstract thought.

But they are not good at using them yet, so they must experiment – and sometimes they use their parents as guinea pigs. Many kids in this age view conflict as a type of self-expression and may have trouble focusing on an abstract idea or understanding another's point of view.

Just as when dealing with the tantrums of toddlerhood, parents need to remember their teen's behaviour is "not a personal affront".

They are dealing with a huge amount of social, emotional and cognitive flux and have underdeveloped abilities to cope. They need their parents – those people with the more stable adult brain – to help them by staying calm, listening and being good role models.

"Puberty is the beginning of major changes in the limbic system," referring to the part of the brain that not only helps regulate heart rate and blood sugar levels, but also is critical to the formation of memories and emotions.

Part of the limbic system, the amygdale is thought to connect sensory information to emotional responses. Its development, along with hormonal changes, may provoke newly intense experiences of rage, fear, aggression (including towards oneself), excitement and sexual attraction.

Over the course of adolescence, the limbic system comes under greater control of the prefrontal cortex, the area just behind the forehead, which is associated with planning, impulse control and higher order thought.

As additional areas of the brain start to help process emotion, older teens gain some equilibrium and have an easier time interpreting others. But until then, they often misconstrue their teachers and parents.

"You can be as careful as possible and you still will have tears or anger at times because they will have misunderstood what you have said," she said.

A research says: "As teens become better at thinking abstractly, their social anxiety increases."

Abstract reasoning makes it possible to consider yourself from the eyes of another. Teens may use this new skill to ruminate about what others are thinking of them. In particular, peer approval has been shown to be highly rewarding to the teen brain which may be why teens are more likely to take risks when other teens are around.

"Kids are really concerned with looking cool – but you don't need brain research to tell you that," she said.

Friends also provide teens with opportunities to learn skills such as negotiating, compromise and group planning. "They are practising adult social skills in a safe setting and they are really not good at it at first," says Feinstein. So even if all they do is sit around with their friends, teens are hard at work acquiring important life skills.

✘ ✘ ✘

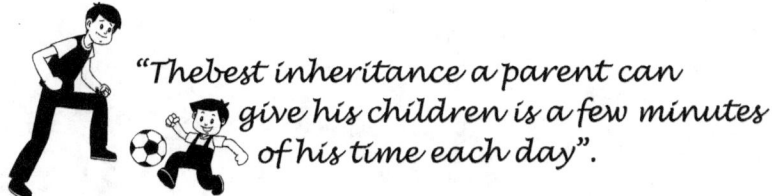

"The best inheritance a parent can give his children is a few minutes of his time each day".

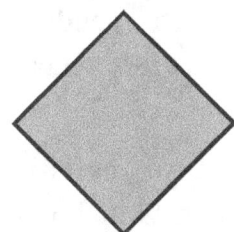

TIPS TO HELP YOUR CHILD THROUGH EARLY ADOLESCENCE

"Spread love everywhere you go; first of all in your house. Give love to your children, to your wife or husband, to a next door neighbour. Let no one ever come to you without leaving better and happier."
~*Mother Teresa*

1. Try to learn as much as you can about early adolescence. Good information can help you make good decisions. Find out the changes you expect during these years. Learn about what goes on in your child's school.

2. Stay involved in your child's life, keeping a watchful eye on both inside and outside of school. A positive relationship with a parent or other adult is the best safeguard your child has as he grows and explores. Find new and different ways to stay involved that work well with your child.

3. Provide both unconditional love and appropriate limits to help your child thrive and feel safe.

4. Talk with your child often about what she considers the most important to her. Include the tough and sensitive subjects. Listen to what she has to say and try to know what she tries to suppress and avoid telling you. Connected children are generally happier and do better in every sphere of life.

5. Hold your child to high but within realistic standards both in school and in life. Let him know that you expect him to work hard, cooperate with teachers and other students and do his best.

6. Show that you value education. Stay in touch with your child's teachers and school officials. Check whether he gets to school on time, completes homework assignments successfully and is signed up for classes required for college.

7. Provide opportunities for your young teen to succeed. Help your child discover and develop her strengths. Success produces confidence.

8. Monitor friendships. Get to know how are your child's friends and their parents. Talk with him about friends, friendship and about choices he makes when with friends.

9. Work with your child to make him/her more aware of the media and how to use it appropriately. Discuss what TV and movies to watch and what computer games to play. Become aware of the music she listens to and the magazines she reads.

10. Try to evolve yourself as a model of good behaviour and fair dealings. The best way to raise a child who is loving, decent and respectful is to live the values and behaviour you hope he will develop.

11. Be alert to major problems, such as drug use, depression or an eating disorder. If the problem is too big to handle alone, get help from some of the many resources available.

12. Hang in there when times are tough. Most youngsters weather the bumps of early adolescence successfully and grow into successful adults. You play a major role in making that happen.

❌❌❌

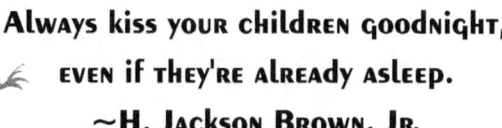

Always kiss your children goodnight,
even if they're already asleep.
~H. Jackson Brown, Jr.

WHAT PARENTS NEED TO KNOW ABOUT TEENS: FACTS, MYTHS AND STRATEGIES

"Parenting now is a two-way relationship where you
learn from each other."
~*Juhi Chawla*

You need to know what's considered normal adolescent behaviour, how to determine whether your child is on a good path, how to encourage his healthy development and how to get help when problems arise. There are many new things influencing teens today, but your parenting role is as crucial today as ever before. Spending time strengthening your relationship with your teen is the best investment in her future, just as it was when she was a child.

In my work with adolescents, I'm often asked by parents, "What do I need to know to help my teen avoid alcohol and other drugs, abusive peers or dating partners and other worries?" News reports remain replete with upsetting stories about injuries and other forms of harm stemming from drinking, driving, partying or bullying— which makes parents all the more concerned. Today's pressures on teens come in different forms than in previous generations, but pressure is pressure, and to a teen it can seem overwhelming at times.

Parents may also feel overwhelmed with the problems and situations teens bring home, especially when some of these didn't exist when they were growing up, like Internet bullying or chat rooms. Many parents feel they would benefit from the advice on how to meet their teens' necessities, how to promote maturity and responsibility, and ways to avoid danger.

It's true that adolescence is the most precarious period of development, especially from ages 16 to 19, and even extending to age 24, when many finish their college or university studies and save a bit of money before leaving (or being gently nudged from) the family nest. After age 16, the combination of greater access to adult privileges such as driving, extended curfews, alcohol and other drugs, empty family homes or even separate living arrangements makes this age ripe for trouble. But, the image of teens as immature, fun seeking and irresponsible is overblown and inaccurate. The vast majority of teens emerge from this period unscathed— especially when their parents or caregivers practise effective parenting and put their utmost to prepare, not scare, their teen for assuming these new responsibilities and the pressures that may accompany them.

As parents, we know that simply letting our teenagers learn for themselves is not a good choice. The risk of injury or long-term health problems that could result is too high. Likewise, simply telling teens they can't do certain things ("Just say no!") doesn't work. Threatening them with consequences ("If I catch you drinking, you'll be grounded for a month!"), or putting up legal, or family, roadblocks to curtail activities are not very effective with teens. We need to help them develop personal strategies, a sense of responsibility, and values that reduce their chances of harm, especially now that they are spending much more time doing things on their own.

We can choose to sit and wait for our teenagers to make mistakes and react to them—usually through punishments or lectures—or we can try to head off problems by being a reliable source of information and support. While we can't make all the choices for them, we can assist them in making the most responsible choices possible. The best way to achieve this goal is to maintain a balance between being sensitive to their desires and needs, yet firm in providing guidance and direction when you should not be yielding to your child's unjustifiable demands.

Keep in mind that adolescence is all about experimentation. Because a certain amount of experimentation is normal, our job as parents is to figure out how to maintain a balance between setting limits (yes— teens need limits) and promoting their independence (yes— teens need to develop their own limits). This balancing act between hanging on and letting go is a major challenge of parenting a teenager.

As the parent of a teen you need information about three key issues:

- You need to know what behaviour is "normal" during adolescence so that you can better understand and guide your teen accordingly. Because none of us is born an expert parent, you might have worked hard to understand your child during infancy and early childhood. Adolescence requires the same amount of effort—if not more!

- You need a basic understanding of how you and your family, in addition to your teen, are experiencing change in their lives. By identifying the challenges that you and your teen face during this time of rapid transition, you will be better prepared to be a source of strength and guidance.

- Finally, you need information on the best ways to be an effective parent during this period of development so that you are strengthening your relationship with your teen and avoiding some of the common "traps".

The objective of this book is to help you have a better understanding of these key issues pertaining to adolescent development, and how your role as a parent can make an important difference in how teens develop the ability to make good choices.

How teens manage their relationships—with family members, with peers and with other important adults—is a key element in determining how they learn to make safe and responsible choices. Ultimately, the process begins with their relationship with you. Now as much as ever, what parents do does matter to their children.

"Teens Need Parents as Much as Young Children Do!!"

✗ ✗ ✗

"Love your children more than your ego.
Love your children enough to allow them to
progress through childhood as non-perfect beings,
who are a work in progress, just like you are."
-Nicholeen Peck

SOME READY TIPS TO MAKE THE PARENTING TASK EASY!!

"I am always trying to evolve, so I like to read
parenting books and things like that."
~*Kourtney Kardashian*

Like infants, adolescents also need the caring of adults. They may be able to talk a good game, but teens are neither emotionally nor physically mature enough to take care of themselves. Despite the generational conflict that sometimes exists between parents and their teen-aged children, parents still serve as the primary role models and primary sources of support for their teen children. By definition, the teen years are years of change.

And change, by definition, is scary. Our teenage children deserve adequate nurturing and attention.

- **Parents provide important role models:** In their search for and struggle to create a personal identity and a sense of self, teens will look to adults whom they admire for skills, attitudes and values that they can imitate. In some cases, teens may copy the fashions and behaviour of contemporary celebrities whose values may not be the kind most parents want their kids to acquire. Parents can become good role models for their teens and exert a deepening influence on their development. The following practical tips may help a parent understand how their own behaviour can positively influence the behaviour of a teenaged child.

• **Talk:** If you want your teen to communicate openly and honestly with you, you must be open and honest with them. Encouraging your teen to talk to you means being attentive and being willing to really listen to them. It also means being prepared to deal honestly and candidly with sensitive subjects like sex and drugs. Avoid being judgmental and eliminate "communication closers" like criticising or sympathising. When engaged in a meaningful discussion with your teen, do not let yourself be distracted or interrupted, which only gives a message that the interruption is more important than what the teen has to say. A good first step will be turning off the TV or putting down the newspaper when your teen wants to talk to you.

- **Display Exemplary Behaviour**: If you want your teen to deal responsibly with alcohol, you need to show them how. Do you drink when you are upset or stressed out? Do you over-indulge? Is drinking a significant part of the home environment? Do you drink to escape? If so, you may be teaching your teen those very behaviours you want to prevent.

- **Trust**: If you want your teen to be trustworthy, you need to demonstrate your trust in him/ her. Teens need limits that are flexible enough to meet their changing needs and permit self-direction. Negotiating limits is a good way to build trust between you and your teenager. Giving your teen responsible choices also helps him or her to become more independent.

- **Respect**: If you want your teen to respect you, you must, in turn, respect him/her.

- **Give Privacy**: Showing respect means avoid encroaching upon their privacy. It means acknowledging and accepting their feelings without trying to change them. It also means respecting the ways - dress, hairstyle, music, and choice of friends - in which a teen is trying to express himself or herself.

- **Support**: Parents must provide physical and emotional support that teens need in this phase of life. The support could be in the form of providing comfort, reassurance, feedback and guidance - just like younger children. Here are some specific ways parents can support their teenaged children.

- **Be Available**: Being physically present isn't enough for your children until you willingly and devoutly listen to them, evince your interest in what's going on in their lives and express your readiness to be helpful whenever you are needed by them.

  Keep your problems to yourself. Teens have a full enough plate already. This means doing what you need to do to take care of yourself.

- **Be Nurturing:** Both verbally and physically. Don't assume that kids know you love them. Frequent saying of "I love you" should be avoided as it gives the sense of sham expression. So you can substitute this saying with a hug or even a tuck up in bed. The bumper sticker's question: "Have you hugged your child today?" applies to teenagers, too.

- **Be Companionable**: Although teens begin to spend more and more time away from home, you can seize opportunities to participate with them in activities they enjoy. It can be as simple as watching a favourite TV show together, following a sports team, cooking a favourite recipe or going to the auto show. Don't be afraid to issue the invitation. Sometimes all a kid is waiting for is to be asked.

- **Be Cautious**: Don't assume the other adults in your teenager's life will clue you in. While your teen's friends may confide in their parents, don't assume these parents will give you the scoop on your child's behaviour. Too often parents fear losing their children's confidence so much that they won't pass information on to other parents. Schools, too, can't be counted on. Guidance counsellors and teachers may have little time to let parents know of difficulties their teen may be facing in school.

- **Be Alert**: Pay attention to the discrepancy between what a teen says and what they do or how they look. Changes in physical appearance can be early warning signs of disorders in sleep, eating patterns or indulgence in drug and alcohol use. Don't ignore what's right before your very eyes.

- **Intervene when necessary.** If you suspect your child is making detrimental choices, let him know you are aware of it and get help. Paediatricians specialising in the field of adolescent medicine can provide assistance, as can psychologists and other counsellors.

✗ ✗ ✗

RESOURCES

"I do think that there's an art form to parenting, and I have nothing but admiration for those who do it well."
~Elizabeth Berg

For various resources like publications, personality test, organisations, websites, etc.,

GullybabaKids.com/blog/adolescent-resources

www.ingramcontent.com/pod-product-compliance
Lightning Source LLC
Chambersburg PA
CBHW051150260626
47170CB00005B/2039